SUBMIT TO ME

THE ATLAS COLLECTION (BOOK 4)

SAPPHARIA MAYER

Ebook ISBN: 978-1-64893-009-6

Audiobook ISBN: 978-1-64893-011-9

Print ISBN: 978-1-64893-010-2

SUBMIT TO ME

AUTHOR'S NOTE

Dear reader,

I am so glad you picked up my book, and I hope you enjoy the story it weaves. Please remember, theses books are works of fiction. The timelines are compressed, the interactions are dramatic and characters often jump into things for want of adventure.

You, dearest reader, live in a reality where the world is often stranger than fiction and a good dominant or submissive is hard to find. When you do find one, it is quickly evident they are imperfect humans who can't read minds, are less observant than one might prefer, and the interaction with them takes time. Like all things in life, communication is the key to any good interaction. The more authentically open you can be with a partner the more fulfilling the relationship.

Remember you are in charge of your life. Use your safe word, let others know where you are, know what aftercare looks like for you, use protection and have fun. The goal is to live in a beautiful safe, sane and consensual relationship with all parties pulling their weight. It is my hope you all find your special someone, just like the characters in my books. **~*Sappharia***

WARNINGS & DISCLAIMERS

WARNING:

This book contains sexually explicit scenes and adult language. It may be considered offensive to some readers. This book is for sale to adults only, as defined by the laws of the country in which you made your purchase.

DISCLAIMER:

Please do not try any new sexual practice, without the guidance of an experienced practitioner. Neither the publisher nor the author will be responsible for any loss, harm, injury, or death resulting from use of the information contained in this book.

CHAPTER ONE

The insistent blare of the phone as it walked across the nightstand in a constant vibration pulled Kade out of the edge of sleep. It screamed its emergency and demanded his attention. He glanced at the clock and noted he'd only lain down less than two hours ago. Fighting instinct, he let the phone continue until it died. He breathed a sigh of relief and punched the pillow. Just as he settled, the phone vibrated again, and he cursed under his breath, rolled over, and grabbed the phone.

"Empyrean Command Center" the bright screen announced the caller. He slid a large thumb across the screen and grit his teeth.

"Kade!" His voice was harsh and hoarse.

He'd run another long shift. As the head of security for the club, it was his job to keep everyone safe. His most recent failure to protect the owner, Alexandra, added to his already heavy burden and guilt.

"Sir, we have a situation." The edge in the voice on the other end of the phone was clear but told him little about the problem.

"Spit it out. I'm in no mood to guess our most recent incident and decide it if is an actual problem or if you all are too incompetent to know the difference."

"Sir, I need you to come to the club ASAP. I'd rather not discuss it on an open line."

Kade ran his hand through his barely-there high and tight. A scowl marred his face.

"I'm twenty mikes out," he acknowledged.

"Roger that."

The line when dead, and Kade rolled to sit up on the edge of the bed. Good thing he'd showered last night; it looked like it would be another long day. He walked over to his closet, grabbing a pair of black BDUs and a club security polo. He took less than five minutes to dress and grab his keys as he headed for the garage.

The bright red Tesla Roadster called to him. He could imagine pushing his irritation through her on the way to the club as he ripped through the gears and took the corners hard.

Instead, he opted for the large black Cadillac Escalade. In one smooth motion, he hit start on the remote and the garage door responded. He slid behind the wheel and pulled out of the driveway. As soon as he was on the road, he hit the accelerator and pushed the large vehicle toward the club he'd left recently.

Ten minutes later, he pulled up at the back gate, which opened immediately in response to his RFID car tag. The long narrow road wasn't as elegant as the main entrance, but the service road provided the perfect vantage point as he approached the club.

From this angle, everything was quiet. The light fog of the morning sat just off the ground, giving the scene an ethereal look. He pulled the SUV up to the parking garage gate and waited for it to respond. Beside him, the security camera panned down, and seconds later the garage door began its descent.

He pulled through the parking structure and backed into the open space marked "Reserved for Security Director."

As soon as the engine died, his door opened. A young man passed a cup of coffee and a radio to him.

"Sit rep," he commanded.

"Sir, a threat was posted on the front door."

"What kind of threat?" Kade asked as he accepted the coffee and climbed out of the driver's seat. He didn't stop moving toward the club door as he heard the SUV's door shut and reverberate around the structure. The thump of boots echoed in his wake as the young man worked to keep up.

Kade stopped and turned. He glared at the man before him.

"I said what kind of threat, boot?" he growled, his irritation sitting right at the surface.

"Someone stabbed a bloody knife into the front door with a threatening note."

Kade turned toward the door, swiped his badge, and headed to the command center.

"Who's on fire watch?"

"Tanner. He's in the command center reviewing the tapes. He's called in all personnel."

"Roger."

He continued through the club as he connected his radio and settled his earpiece, clicking to set the current channel. His mind struggled to catch up with the situation on the ground.

Kade clicked the button and spoke into his mic.

"Radio check," he called and released the button.

"Five by five," a voice answered in response.

Satisfied his radio was in good working order, he took a long swig of his black coffee, thankful for the dark elixir's power to put him back on his feet. He desperately needed sleep. Between his constant nightmares and the evolving security situation surrounding the club, he never seemed to catch enough time before something else needed his immediate attention.

His heavy boots echoed off the marble foyer tile as he made his way through the club.

"Does anyone have eyes on Kade?" The radio crackled in his ear, and he groaned inwardly.

"Go for Kade."

"What's your twenty?"

"Head to Command, over."

"Kade, this is Command. Code Yellow at the front gate."

"Copy that. Redirecting."

He turned toward Dean. He was new to the team, and everyone referred to him as boot.

"With me," he commanded and pivoted to the side door. He didn't want to disturb the site of investigation.

"On your six, Sir."

The two men walked out through the side service entrance of the large house. The brisk morning air helped him clear the last remnants of sleep from his mind. Years of military training forced an automatic calm as the adrenaline coursed through him. As they approached the circular driveway, he looked out toward the gate. White specks of vehicles pulled near the entrance.

Kade grabbed the small tablet housed in his side pocket. A couple taps later, the screen lit up with the image from the front gate. Three news vans were setting up. Satellite dishes reached toward the sky.

"Whisky Tango Foxtrot," he swore under his breath and turned toward the front door.

Someone had buried a KA-BAR knife deep in the center of the right double door. Thick plops of blood dripped from the handle, marring the marble entrance. Under the knife's tip, a piece of paper fluttered in the breeze.

"Command to Kade." The radio crackled.

"Go for Kade."

"Sir, we've got incoming black and whites."

Frustration tightened every muscle in his body. The situation was spinning out of control faster than he could get a handle on it.

"Command, did you call them?"

"Negative."

"This is becoming a cluster fuck," he grumbled, and then clicked the button on his radio. "Command, get Gabriel on the horn. This situation is FUBAR."

"Copy that."

Kade lifted the tablet. With a swipe, he aimed it at the front door and worked to take pictures from every angle to study later. If it was from Edmund, then at least it meant Alexandra was safe. On the other hand, the news outlets in front of the club also meant there was an incoming public relations nightmare.

"Black and whites are demanding entrance." The radio crackled.

"Give me three mikes and let them through," he called back.

"Roger."

He turned toward Dean.

"Stay frosty. It's about to get intense."

The young man nodded. He'd hired Dean as a favor to a friend. When he tried to join the military, he'd been rejected based on an undiagnosed knee deformity. The kid needed structure and discipline in his life, and Kade had taken him under his wing. He'd learned quickly, and Kade had high hopes he'd be a valuable asset to the team.

"Incoming." The voice crackled over the radio.

"Roger," Kade replied. "All stations, this is Kade. Impose radio silence. Over."

The radio echoed with several calls of "Copy that" and "Roger," then fell silent as the police cars pulled into the circular drive.

KADE PULLED HIS PHONE OUT OF HIS POCKET AS HE WATCHED two unmarked cars roll down the driveway toward him while two marked cars stayed at the gate. With two quick taps, he pulled up Samantha's phone number and waited for it to connect.

"There better be a good reason for this call," her sleepy voice sang through the line.

"You better turn on the TV. I think we will need your expertise—fast," Kade replied simply.

"What's going on?" The sudden alertness in her tone gave him a moment of control in his spiraling world.

"Just turn on the television. You're the public relations person. I think we're getting ready to have a real problem."

"You've got to give me more details than that, man," she demanded.

"Later. Just do your job," he interrupted and ended the call as the cars rolled to a stop in front of him.

The captain of the police force stepped out of the first car and walked up the stairs.

"Looks like y'all have a bit of a situation, Kade." The older man smiled and held out his hand. Because of the clientele and the nature of the business, he'd worked closely with the local police department for the last several years.

"Indeed," Kade answered noncommittally.

The sound of a door shutting brought both men's attention to a woman stepping out of the other car. She was small, almost fragile, in the looming shadow of the large house. Her suit hugged every curve of her well-toned body. His eyes lingered down to her bare legs and back up again. There was something about her that pulled on Kade's need to protect and set him on edge.

"This is Detective Lawson. She'll be running our investigation," the captain said as the woman made her way up the front marble stairs.

When she reached the top, she stuck out her hand.

"And you are?" she asked.

Kade's large hand engulfed hers and their touch sent a buzz straight to his groin, making him scowl.

"Kade. Director of Security."

Her eyebrow quirked, and her eyes narrowed at his short, direct answer.

"Well, Kade." She tried out his name and scrunched her nose like it wasn't quite right. "We got an anonymous call there was a possible murder on the property."

"A murder? Really?"

"Yes. Do you mind if I have a look around?" Her tone was even, giving away nothing.

"Actually, I mind."

"You know, this can go down easy for both of us or I can make it a shit show," she challenged.

"I see," Kade replied evenly. For a long time they stared each other down. Her assumption of control was hot as hell. He continued to look down at the diminutive woman. The air practically sizzled with tension when both refused to back down.

He broke eye contact and reached for the button on his earpiece. Out of the corner of his eye, he saw her take a mental victory lap as her shoulders straightened. The move pushed her pert breasts forward under her jacket, and he internally moaned.

Get it together, he scolded himself and pushed the button.

"All teams secure comms on Channel 7. Secure posts 3, 7, 9, 12, and 15. Secure comms only," he said into the radio.

He watched her face fall as he looked up.

"Now. How can I help you today, Detective?" he said in a neutral tone that belied the mass of things running through his body.

Kade waited a long heartbeat before she spoke again.

"Shall we start over?" she asked, forcing a smile across her face.

He loved the fire in her eyes. There was something about her that made him want to challenge her and watch her rise to meet it.

"Sure."

"Mr. Kade, I'm Detective Jessica Lawson. Someone called in an anonymous tip and told us there was a bloody knife and a possible murder on these grounds. I'd like your permission to investigate these allegations so we can both get on with our day." She let a slight smile play across her mouth.

At six foot two, he was almost a foot taller than her, but the confidence and authority told him she wasn't intimidated by their difference in size.

"You look young to be a detective," he said, the words rolling off his tongue without thought.

"Yep. A small, delicate, fragile flower just needing a big, strong man to protect me," she said in a sickly sweet tone.

Embarrassment rushed through him.

"I didn't mean to..." he started.

"Yes, you did. Just like every male before you." She shook her head. "Now if you are quite done with your self-important evaluation of my skills based solely on my size, can we get on with this investigation? I've got more important things to do than to have a 'my dick is bigger than yours' contest. Besides, I can strap mine on in the necessary size and shape. Unfortunately, for you, yours is original equipment and can't be altered to suit, so I hope it's a good size."

With that, she let her eyes dip down to his crotch for a long, lingering look. He felt his cock grow hard under her scrutiny and breathed a sigh of relief when she looked up again.

"And yes, in fact, mine are brass. Are yours?" She smirked.

Beside him, the captain laughed at the exchange.

"Do you let all your detectives talk to people like this?" Kade looked over at him.

"Don't think you can handle it, big guy?" The captain slapped him on the back and chuckled.

Kade rolled his eyes and looked back down at the detective.

"What do you want to do from here?"

The loaded question made his mind go to all the things he'd like to do with her behind this door. He shook his head at his wayward thoughts, shoving them out of his way in an attempt to rein in the sudden fire in his libido.

"Let me get my forensics team in here and collect evidence. Then search the grounds to see if there's been an actual crime or if this is all an elaborate hoax to bring media attention."

Kade ran a frustrated hand through his hair.

"If we find nothing, I'll make a press statement and scatter the roaches," she said with a shrug. "Or I can walk out there right now, tell them the situation is under investigation, and we're going for a search warrant. I'm sure your clientele will love the constant media attention and the fear of being recognized as they come through those gates." She pointed toward the gate and the building media presence he knew was already there. "Ball's in your court, Mr. Kade."

"Just Kade."

"Say again." She looked up at him.

The sparkle in her pale gray, almost silver eyes, took him aback. He shook his head to regain his composure.

"My name is Kade, just Kade," he growled, his own frustration clear.

"Okay, just Kade. Shall we get this show on the road?"

"Go ahead and bring in your forensics team, Ma'am. Then you can go tell the media it was all a hoax."

"Fantastic," she said with a triumphant smile, but her tone remained even and deadpan. Jessica picked up her radio and issued the order.

Kade punched a new secure channel into his own radio as he watched her.

"Let the forensics vehicle through, Command."

"Copy that," replied a disembodied voice.

"I'll let you get on with it then. Dean, here, will get you anything you need." He nodded toward the young man who'd followed him out earlier.

"Captain. Detective Lawson," he said as he nodded to them both and walked down the stairs.

After that encounter, he needed a cold shower, but first he needed to find out exactly what was going on around here.

CHAPTER TWO

Jessica stared at Kade's retreating tight backside as he walked away. There was something about the man she found infuriating and hot, all at the same time. She reprimanded herself and turned to find Captain Jones watching her.

"Yes, Sir?" she asked, quirking an eyebrow.

"That's one way to make an introduction." He smirked.

The young man assigned to her shifted back and forth on the balls of his feet beside them.

"Captain, I didn't get where I am by being some soft woman who waits for a man to take the lead. He either lets us in to do our job or I have to do more paperwork, which means I'll run more overtime on your already tight budget."

The captain shook his head. "Tread a little lighter on this one. The money that flows through this place is not insignificant, nor is the political power they wield in our nation's capitol," he admonished lightly.

"No offense, Sir. I don't care how those cake eaters in Washington get their freak on. Either this is a hoax and someone is harassing them or someone is dead. That's my job. From top to bottom. You schmooze the money. I'll see if there's a body," Jessica retorted.

"Watch your step, Detective," he said and started down the stairs.

"Yes, Sir."

The forensics van pulled into the driveway to her left, and the captain headed off in the same direction as Kade. Around her, doors popped open and slammed in a staccato as the team formed.

"What do we got, Detective?" a middle-aged man asked as he walked up the stairs toward her.

"Honestly, I don't have a clue. On-site security says there's nothing more than this knife stabbed into a door, but the anonymous tip says there's a possible murder on site. Let's process this immediate scene. I'll work on getting access inside. Then we'll set up a search team to cover the outside and any outbuildings."

"Sounds good," he acknowledged, then turned to his team. "Okay, folks, let's get to work. Process everything as a murder investigation."

Jessica walked down the steps to give the team room, and Dean followed on her heels. She watched as bright yellow crime scene tape roped off the large marble front steps. On one side of the portico, a photographer snapped pictures, while another team member placed evidence markers.

"How long have you worked here, Dean?" she asked as she watched the proceedings.

"Just over six months, Ma'am," he responded without confidence.

"Has anything like this happened before?"

"Not like this."

She let a long silence linger in the air. Just enough to make him believe the scene distracted her but not long enough to disengage the conversation.

"But something has happened before," she finally asked, maneuvering the question toward her curiosity.

"The... um... nature of the club... um... can cause some... um... problems," he stuttered.

"Are you uncomfortable with the nature of the activities going on here?" she asked curiously.

"Um... at first. It can all be a bit intimidating," he replied shyly.

"Do you enjoy watching?"

He shifted his weight and rubbed his hands together as he fidgeted with a ring on his finger.

She smiled to herself. More than once she'd seen a man fidget under her scrutiny. It was a game of cat and mouse she used both in play and work. Sometimes it was all about fun, and others it was deadly serious.

"It's my job to make sure everyone is safe, and the activities are consensual," he finally replied with more confidence.

Jessica nodded.

"It must be a tough job. All of these heightened emotions in such a tight space. I can't imagine how hard it is to be surrounded with all these activities and stay focused on the job at hand," she said as a slight smile lifted at the corners of her mouth. "So to speak."

She watched Dean nod out of her periphery.

"I've learned a lot. Kade is a good trainer—tough but good."

"Tough? How so?" she inquired.

Dean shrugged and thought about his answer.

"His standards are high and demanding. I guess they reflect the club owner's expectation, but I don't know. She's not been here for months."

This piece of information piqued her interest, but she schooled her expression as if it were of no consequence.

"Is this unusual? Is she usually gone for long stretches of time?"

"I don't think so, but I don't really know. Like I said, I'm new to the organization."

Jessica nodded, taking a mental note of the anomaly.

"Does the club owner... What did you tell me her name was?" Jessica asked, letting a tinge of confusion paint her tone.

"Alexandra," he supplied automatically.

"Yes, Alexandra. Thank you. I presume Alexandra has her own security detail unless this type of thing is rare."

"She gave her last one the slip, so I don't know."

She kept her eyes forward on the scene investigation in front of her. Her mind spun with a thousand questions as puzzle pieces formed.

Beside her, Dean shifted uncomfortably and pushed the earpiece against his ear.

"Ma'am, if you'll excuse me, I need to attend to something."

Jessica nodded without looking him.

"Please tell Kade I'd like to speak with him, and I need a copy of all the security tapes for the last twenty-four hours." She smiled and looked up at him.

"Yes, Ma'am." He nodded curtly and turned to walk away.

Above her, the security camera motor whirled to life as it tilted in her direction. With a smile, she looked directly into the camera and waved.

She'd gotten someone's attention and that meant there was more to this puzzle than met the eye.

JESSICA LET HER GAZE TAKE IN THE VAST CLUB GROUNDS. Everything around her appeared immaculately maintained, and from the number of cameras she counted, well monitored.

Something about this situation bothered her. It appeared to be a hoax. Harassment most likely meant to threaten a more alternative lifestyle. Such things often happened, depending on who was in power. Recent political changes made people bold, and there had been an increase in this type of behavior.

She made her way around the scene, letting questions form in her mind as she looked at it from different perspectives. Until she understood the motive, the rest would be difficult to unwrap. Jessica suspected the private club security knew something, and she was determined to find out what.

As she moved around the scene, she noted that the pan and tilt cameras followed her movements. At first she thought it was based on motion, but she realized the cameras didn't follow the other members of the team.

"Detective?" Dan, a young forensics investigator, called to her from a small walkway near the building.

Jessica looked up and noticed he was squatting. Something on the ground held his attention.

"What is it, Dan?" she asked as she approached.

"I don't know that it is anything, but there's a fresh footprint here in the grass. It looks like someone stumbled off the walkway and landed in the soft dirt."

Jessica tucked her suit skirt under her as she squatted next to the investigator.

"It looks like a bare foot, but that makes no sense. Why would anyone be barefoot in front of a club like this one?" he speculated aloud and looked closer.

"Wait, there's a tread mark. I bet it's one of those barefoot running shoes."

She leaned forward and took in the scene.

"Do you think the print is male or female?"

"Hard to tell. It's not a large print, but it's not tiny either," he said and glanced over at her feet before he abruptly brought his gaze back to the footprint.

"It could go either way and it could be unrelated," he continued. "I'd like to take a casting, just in case."

"Sounds good," she replied and stood up. "I will see if we can look at the rest of the grounds."

Dan nodded but didn't look up as she stepped away.

She followed the pathway to the edge of the large house as it continued to bend between the house and what appeared to be a guesthouse.

"Is there something I can help you with, Ma'am?" A deep voice startled her, and she whipped around.

Her eyes climbed up the impossibly tall man in front of her until her neck could go back no farther.

"I'm looking for Kade."

"He's inside talking with your captain," he stated simply.

"You mean my captain is trying to calm the money while we figure out what is going on here."

The man chuckled. "It would entertain Kade to be considered the 'money.'" He smiled down at her.

"How many of you are there?" she asked, trying to keep a tally of the number of private security personnel.

"Of me? There's only one."

Jessica exhaled. "Let me rephrase. How many security personnel are on site?"

"At this moment, there are six club security personnel on-site." His short, specific answer frustrated her, especially when she saw a smile pull at his mouth.

"So the club uses six security type?"

"Ma'am, you asked how many were on-site. I've provided you with the information you requested."

"Indeed," she acknowledged and searched for a new tactic. "Are all of you former military?"

He nodded. "Except for the boot."

"Ah, you're former Marine."

The man quirked an eyebrow, and she smiled.

"Now, where might I find Kade?"

CHAPTER THREE

"**K**ade." The captain's voice echoed around the lush foyer as his shoes clicked across the marble.

Kade pivoted at the sound of his name but continued to give orders into the mic of his earpiece. When the captain was within a few feet, he fell silent and forced a smile across his face.

"What can I do for you, Captain?"

The two men had a long history together. When Alexandra had first opened the club, it was imperative they made quick and fast friends with the local law enforcement. Too much of what went on within these walls pushed the edges of proprietary and the law. It didn't matter if the laws were outdated; anything on the books could be applied at any moment given the right enemy and political climate. Since then, they'd contracted out to the beat cops on the force when they needed extra security for an event or to give his own team some well-needed time off.

"You can start by telling me what is going on around here." His tone was respectful but firm.

"To be honest, I wish I knew."

He rubbed the back of his neck in frustration.

"I was here until close last night. Left the team to fend for themselves until later this afternoon and headed home for sleep I desperately need."

"You look like hell," the captain acknowledged.

"Thanks," Kade replied dryly. "What's up with your new pup? Is she all bark and no bite?"

"You mean Detective Lawson?"

Kade nodded.

"Her bite is far worse than her bark. She wasn't kidding around out there. That one is intense. When she gets a bone between her teeth, she'll let go when she wants to let go and not before."

"Great," Kade groaned. "Just what I needed."

"Actually, I think she's exactly what you need. Something's wrong around here, and you need help."

"How do you mean?"

"Don't play stupid. We've been at this for a while now. Alexandra doesn't just take off and leave her precious club without someone at the helm."

"I'm at the helm," Kade spat.

"You're at the helm out of force and need. It's the last place you want to be, and we both know it."

"Regardless, this current situation is just a security issue. My team can handle it. There's no reason to waste your resources."

"Mind if we look around then? Satisfy our investigative curiosity?"

"You know I can't do that. It violates half a dozen rights to privacy and I'm still getting up to speed on the situation."

"Come on. Give us something here. We need to explain it to the frenzy out front unless you enjoy this kind of media attention."

"Sadist," Kade chided.

"Just now figuring that one out, huh?" The captain chuckled.

"No. I've seen you play. I see all." Kade gestured around the grand hall with his tablet.

"I think the power's going to your head."

He shook his head. "Not even close. I can quip about it all day. The power I wield is because I'm good at it and it keeps the most important people in my world safe. The rest of it is heavy. I do not understand why Alexandra does it."

"We all have our reasons."

"Don't I know it."

The tablet in Kade's hand pinged, and he glanced down.

"Looks like your pit bull wants in my doghouse," Kade quipped.

"You might as well let her in or she'll find a way around the fence. Besides, I really think she can help here. You need to trust her."

"There's a hard ask."

"Think of it as a favor. I make sure the front porch roaches are cleared away, and you work with her on whatever the hell it is that you're trying to hide from the world. Fair?"

Kade ran a hand through his hair as he stared at her image on the screen of his tablet.

"Fine," he mumbled. "Take a team and do an outside sweep. I'll send two of my guys with you to open doors and such."

"Okay. Good luck with Detective Lawson. You'll need it," the captain said as he smiled and turned on his heels.

He issued the commands into this radio and watched the activity from the camera feeds.

"Just what I need," he mumbled out loud, engrossed in camera feeds.

"I'm sure I am, but we'll get to that later."

Her quiet voice echoed through around him in an almost ethereal tone. His head snapped up to meet her calculating stare.

"Shall we get started?"

Images formed in his mind at her question and all the things he'd like to get started with her. He needed to get himself under control or this would be a long day.

"This way," he commanded as he turned and walked toward his office.

He heard the soft click of her heels across the floor. Her footfalls

19

barely echoed around the room, yet something about her sheer presence was enormous. They worked their way back through the maze of the club until they came to his office.

"Can I get you anything to drink, Detective?" Kade asked as they passed through the door.

"Water, please."

He glanced over his shoulder to tell her to have a seat when he noticed her small frame lowering itself into the largest chair of the conversation area. A low growl emitted from his chest, and his hands balled. That was his chair. Everything else in the arrangement was placed to make others know who was in charge when they were having a discussion, and right now she was sitting in his chair. How dare she walk into his house and presume to take over?

With a great deal of effort, he grabbed two bottles of water from the small refrigerator under his desk and took two deep breaths to settle his rising agitation. Then he turned and walked back toward the seating area, placing a bottle of water on the small table beside Jessica and taking a seat across from her on the leather loveseat.

He watched as she scribbled furiously on the small pad of paper in her hand. She didn't look up or acknowledge him, and each second that clicked by made his blood boil.

Kade cleared his throat loudly.

"Mr. Kinkaid, when I am done with my notes we can talk, but an attempt to interrupt me will not go well for either of us," she said without looking up or even pausing her pen.

How dare she? Kade wanted to scream. Who the hell did this little spit of a woman think she was walking into his house and demanding he wait?

Every muscle in him tensed and released in a rolling wave. The action did little to slake his need to punch something, but discipline and patience were drilled into him at a bone-deep level. Just when he didn't think he could sit still another minute, she placed the notebook in her lap and looked up.

"Tell me why you don't think this is a hoax?" Her penetrating stare would unnerve a lesser person, and still it took everything in Kade to meet it.

"There's nothing to suggest otherwise." He batted the answer back at her.

"You wired this place for sound. There are enough cameras to cover every square inch. Based on that, tell me who planted the knife on your front door."

Kade stilled at the question. His team was combing through the tapes, and they'd come up empty so far. In addition, there was twenty-four-hour surveillance. The operation's center should have known the minute the incident happened, but lately there'd been too many breaches and issues. He'd already worked through his own doubts about his team, but each situation seemed to be a step ahead of them.

"My team is looking at the footage now. We should know shortly," Kade spat, scrubbing his face with his hands.

"What time did you leave last night?" Jessica asked.

Her expressionless face gave nothing away, yet there was something else in the mix Kade couldn't quite put his finger on.

CHAPTER FOUR

J essica watched him from the oversized chair. It would fit his large form perfectly, but it swallowed her whole. She felt like a child in a grown-up chair but refused to let it show. The minute she'd seen the seating arrangement, she knew which one she'd choose. He meant it to intimidate and set a power tone to anyone who sat in this conversational area.

Across from her, she watched the well-controlled emotions roll through the director of security. There was something about him. If someone forced her to profile it, she'd call it guilt, but there was no evidence he was guilty of anything in this situation. So her only alternative was to dig deeper and find out what was going on here.

"You look tired," she observed out loud.

Kade nodded. "It's been a trying day, and it's still early."

"How about you let me help? We can go over security tapes together. If it's a hoax, then I'm out of your hair. If it's not a hoax, then I can lend a hand to help solve whatever is going on around here."

Kade took a deep breath and stared at her.

"I appreciate the offer, Detective, but we've got the situation under control."

"Call me Jessica," she offered.

"Excuse me?" Confusion etched Kade's face.

"Call me Jessica. Detective sounds stuffy and formal," she said with a smile. "Mr. Kinkaid, if I might make an observation, we might get further."

"I don't think I could stop you if I wanted to, Det... Jessica."

"True enough," she laughed.

The change in her tone caused Kade to visibly relax, and she smiled.

"Your office is small for a director of a department, but I'm banking it was your choice. If I were to guess, the operation center is right through the door on the far wall. The proximity to your team is important to you. You work as a unit, and it is something you want to foster."

Across from her, Kade shifted in his seat.

"An easy observation based on my position," he agreed.

"The chair I'm sitting in is normally yours, and you hate that I am in it. It is a seat of power. Meant to convey a message of non-questioning authority, although I'm sure my small frame just makes it look like a giant clown chair."

Kade chuckled at her statement.

"Currently, you are in a position of power and control, but it isn't one you'd choose or desire. The weight of it is heavy, and you prefer following, carrying out higher orders rather than making them yourself. However, you are fiercely loyal and protective to those in such positions."

She let her observations linger in the air for a long moment. Kade's stare hardened, and he started to stand.

"Sit down, Mr. Kinkaid," Jessica commanded in a non-threatening tone. "I'm not here to take your position, power or control. I'm here to help. This is your house, and I am the guest. However, my skill set might serve the situation well."

"You make an awful lot of presumptions, Detective." Kade's tone was harsh. He leaned forward and rested his elbows on his knees.

"The question is—am I wrong, Mr. Kinkaid?"

His penetrating stare unnerved her. Behind it was raw power. It would be a stupid move not to respect it, but she refused to back down. The thick tension was nearly suffocating. Neither gave up an inch of their well-gained territory. For a long moment, Jessica thought she'd pushed him too far. More than once in her life, she'd been called opinionated, tenacious, and bitchy. None of them were meant as a compliment, but each one made her push harder to prove herself. She would be damned if this hulk of a man would take her knees out from under her. Especially when she genuinely wanted to help.

There was an odd vulnerability in his eyes. Right behind the fierceness and chest beating. Something about him pulled at her. Maybe if she solved this case, she'd fix it and be able to move on with another one in the bag.

Neither one of them backed down, and this stalemate needed an end.

"Well?" she finally asked.

Jessica watched in amazement when Kade lowered his eyes to the floor in concession. The tautness in his frame did not lax. Each movement was a thought until he once again looked up at her. She refused to move her gaze until he verbally gave in to her.

"What, pray tell, are your special set of skills?" Kade quipped and leaned back against the loveseat.

"People," Jessica replied flatly.

"People aren't skills, though I would agree they all think they are special."

She gave him a genuine smile. For the first time, she released the tips of her toes from the floor and let her feet dangle as she shifted in the oversized chair.

"I read people. Observe the situations. Understand motives. Figure out puzzles. Try to see what makes them tick."

"So you're a profiler," Kade observed.

"Not by training. People simply interest me."

"Do I interest you, Detective?" Kade asked, staring at her pointedly.

Jessica's heart skipped a beat. Everything about this man interested her. From the first irritated words at their meeting on the porch, she'd tried to figure out why everything about him felt incongruent. Her body refused to ignore the obvious problem in their situation, but she blatantly disregarded it.

"Everyone interests me, Mr. Kinkaid. Do you think you should draw more or less of my interest?" she volleyed.

It was her turn to watch him shift uncomfortably. She could just imagine him bound in rope. Those muscles straining against the bright white lines. Controlled strength waiting for her next command. Jessica wanted to shake her head to banish the wayward thoughts but refused to give up the upper hand.

"You are quite the woman," he finally said, avoiding the question.

"So I've been told," Jessica replied with a slight nod. "But you didn't answer my question."

"Are you always this tenacious?"

"We are just getting to know each other, Mr. Kinkaid. There's nothing tenacious about my actions other than a bit of persistence because of your refusal to answer the simplest of questions."

Kade chuckled.

"I'm not all that interesting. My job is to sit in the background and insert my big, dumb body in the way when the situation calls for it."

"On that one, we will agree to disagree for now."

He nodded in acquiescence and smiled back at her.

"How about I go take care of those front porch roaches before the cake eaters stir this town into an unnecessary frenzy? In return, you'll talk to your team, pull together the information, and write up your conclusion. We'll get back together in two days and go over your report and those surveillance tapes. Sound good?"

"Are you always this demanding?"

"That wasn't a demand; it was a statement of how this will proceed."

"I see," Kade replied.

"Do you?"

"Yes, Ma'am," Kade said with a nod.

"Now we're getting somewhere."

Jessica pushed forward and slid out of the oversized chair. She reached into the inside pocket of her jacket and pulled out a business card.

"Here's my contact information. If you need anything, don't hesitate to reach out. Once we find the depth of this situation, we'll know how best to proceed. For now, let me go deal with the press, if I can."

Kade stood, towering over her, and took the card.

"Let me walk you out."

"I can find my way, Mr. Kinkaid. Besides, you've got a lot of work to do before I get back here. I have a feeling you're already behind the eight ball, and you know it."

She nodded up at him, grabbed the water bottle, and headed for the door.

JESSICA MADE HER WAY BACK THROUGH THE CLUB. HER encounter with Kade had unsettled her in a way few people accomplished. Something about him pulled on her and the way the words "Yes, Ma'am" fell from his lips made her wet. She could just imagine him on his knees in front of her with his face buried in the apex of her legs.

Get it together! she admonished herself.

"How'd it go?" The question snapped her out of the wayward thoughts, and she turned toward her captain's voice.

"We've come to a mutual understanding," she replied smoothly as she looked up at him.

"A mutual understanding? You mean you demanded he follow your lead, brow beat him until he complied, and called it a victory?" the captain said with a chuckle.

"I do not brow beat anyone, Captain. I merely persuade them to see it my way and reward compliance as appropriate."

"You mean aggressively persuade," he corrected.

"Are you saying I'm a bitch?" Jessica asked pointedly.

"There's nothing bitchy about you, Detective, but we both know you'll strong arm anyone to get what you want or need."

"I learned from the best men in the business," she returned.

"Yep. It's what makes you so damn good."

"Careful, you're skirting all the politically correct lines these days."

"What are you going to do, turn me in to HR?" he quipped.

"Not on your life. I don't have a problem being part of this organization, and I can hold my own."

"There's an understatement. I think half the department is intimidated by you."

Jessica shrugged. "When you're good at what you do, the situations speak for themselves," she said with a smile.

"Oh, and you've even picked up the cockiness of the men around you."

"No, I'm not cocky."

"Sounds like it to me, Detective."

"No, Captain, I'm arrogant."

"What's the difference? Cocky, arrogant—same same."

"I dare to disagree. Cocky just flaunts it around and acts like they know stuff. Arrogance can back it all up—it's also known as confidence in this day and age."

The captain chuckled and shook his head.

"Besides, I'm a faster draw than most of the department, and I have a good eye for a headshot. I think they are more afraid of me losing it once a month than anything else."

"Glad you said it and not me."

Jessica smiled at him. She liked the easy camaraderie of many of her superiors. She worked her ass off to make them proud of her and accept her like they would any man on the team. At her slight height, she fought harder than anyone else to prove her worth. Every single thing had to be better than everyone else, no matter their advantage.

"So you seemed chummy with the director of security. What can you tell me about his place?" she asked, letting her hand sweep around the vast foyer.

"You mean Kade?"

"Yes," she replied with a raised eyebrow. Jessica knew exactly when the captain was dodging her question.

"Kade and I go way back. The company that owns this place approached the department when they were searching for a location. They... skirt the edge of propriety and in some case the law, no matter how outdated."

"So you what? Help them color inside the lines? Keep their 'edgy' activities in the bag? Supply security for them when they run short?" Jessica pushed.

"Actually, all the above. There are very powerful people who blow off steam in this place."

"Ah, so money talks."

"Of course it does. Don't be naïve, Detective."

"Oh, I wasn't. I just wanted to hear you say it." She smiled. "Do you enjoy your shifts here?"

"You're stepping into a very personal area," the Captain warned.

"All right, all right," Jessica said with her hands raised. "I wanted to know what it was like. I've never been in a place like this, and it's rather... intriguing."

"That's one way to put it," the Captain agreed.

"Well, since I'll get nothing else from you, I guess I'll just have to press Mr. Kinkaid," she said with a grin.

"Leave the boy alone. Do your job and don't go nosing in things which don't concern you," he warned.

"Boy? Did you see him? There's nothing boyish about him. He's huge."

"Only because you're so—" He paused.

"What? Slight? Short? Small? Vertically challenged?"

"Well, yeah."

"Humph. On that note, I have a bunch of white trucks to clear out of here and provide cover for this place of 'mystery'—or should I refer to it like the media does and call it a 'sex club'? That sounds far more torrid, don't you think?"

Jessica spun on her heels without waiting for a reply and headed toward the door she'd originally entered.

Flashbulbs caught her attention from the right, and she worked to keep her face in a neutral expression. In front of her, someone put a small crate behind the podium. She wanted to roll her eyes, but she knew without it, she wouldn't even be seen behind the large array of microphones.

Jessica stepped up to the microphone and took a deep breath as a hush fell across the crowd.

"Good afternoon. I am Detective Lawson, on behalf of the Loundon County Sheriff's department. The purpose of the press conference is to address an anonymous tip called into multiple media outlets and our department in the early hours this morning. The anonymous tip alluded to the fact a homicide was committed on the grounds of the Empyrean property in the pre-dawn hours. Based on our current investigation, an extensive search of the ground and lack of evidence, it is the opinion of this department that no immediate felonious crime was committed. If further evidence presents itself, we will follow the necessary leads.

"I'll open it up to a few questions. Aileen."

"Detective Lawson, what does the Sheriff's Office believe is the motivation to his act of vandalism?"

"There is no current person or motive. Margret?"

"If there's no crime, whose blood was on the knife?"

"Our forensics team is doing an analysis of the scene, so I can't speak to it at this time. Jim?"

"Do you think this is a hate crime based on the type of business which is run on this property?"

"There is no current evidence which points to a hate crime, but we are not ruling out the possibility at this time. Bob?"

"Do you think someone is stalking a member or employee?"

Jessica paused at the question. It seemed completely out of left field. Nothing about the tip or the scene suggested anything to do with stalking, so why would a reporter ask such a pointed question? She collected herself and took a mental note to follow up with Kade at their meeting in two days.

"There's nothing to suggest anyone is being stalked, hunted, hated, or targeted. At this point, we consider it an act of vandalism."

The crowd in front of her clamored for more questions, but she was done with this circus.

"Thank you all very much for your concern. That's all the questions we have time for today."

In front of her, the crowd surged, but she stepped off the wooden crate and disappeared behind the podium. Sometimes there were advantages to her small stature.

She pulled out the pad of paper and pen from her inside jacket pocket and scribbled down a single word: Stalked? Beside it she wrote the reporter's name and news organization who'd asked the odd question. As she made her way back toward the front gate, a thousand questions cluttered her mind in an attempt to form threads through the information.

Something didn't add up, but she couldn't quite put her finger on it. *Like, where was the owner of the club? Was she on vacation or often absent? Based on some of the comments it didn't seem this was normal. And why did Kade feel guilty? What was he hiding? Had there really been a homicide here, and he'd killed the owner and tried to cover it up? Was this about money or power?*

Each question spawned a new one. Some of them made logical

31

sense while others didn't tie into her first impression. Jessica walked back to her car with more questions than answers. With a final look up at the imposing house, she climbed into her unmarked car and headed back to the station.

CHAPTER FIVE

K ade paced his office. The stress of the day made him want to punch something in his frustration.

Reece wasn't answering his damn phone. The news organizations were all over the front gate broadcasting on every channel, hoping to produce the next big DC scandal. Alexandra was in hiding because she was being stalked by a deranged member of the club with more money than the GDP of a small country. A bloody knife had been slammed into the front door of the club with a threatening note. The world was going to hell, and he felt like the conductor of the train.

If that wasn't all bad enough, the sexy as sin Detective Lawson had strode into his office, took his chair, and acted like she could lift the world. Her slight stature made every protective bone in his body go on high alert. Those eyes, the set of her jaw, and her arrogance threatened to demolish anyone who thought they could take her on. He didn't know if he wanted to grab her and throw her over his knee to teach her a lesson or fall to his own to see if she was really all that and then some. Either way, just the thought of her had his cock throbbing in his jeans.

Kade slammed a fist on his desk and reached for the phone, punching the screen harder than necessary.

"Gabriel," the voice on the other end responded after the second ring.

"It's about fucking time you answered the phone," Kade growled in a release of pent-up stress.

"I've been busy," Reece responded flatly.

"Oh, I'm sure it's been so hard being down in that cozy little Caribbean island getting your groove on."

"Well, someone has a burr up his ass today."

Kade sighed and ran a hand through his hair. His normal calm, cool, collected demeanor was fraying around the edges.

"We've had a situation at the club."

"Is everyone okay? Was it serious?" Reece asked calmly, but the edge in his voice spoke volumes.

"Everyone's fine. However, there's quite a media storm."

"The suspense is killing me, spit it out already," Reece deadpanned.

"A bloody knife was stabbed into the front door of the club. There was a note under it."

"Do I even want to know what it said?"

"Yeah. 'If I can't have you, then I will destroy you.'"

Reece seethed in anger on the other in of the line. "That son of a bitch!"

"Do you have an account of..."

A scream punched through the phone. Anger and fear fought for dominance. It was his suggestion that had put them on that small island. It seemed to be the safest option given the circumstances and he was hoping he hadn't just heard his next mistake.

"What the fuck is going on, Reece?" he demanded. "Is Atlas okay?"

"Yes. Someone in this house failed to disconnect the television in her room," he growled.

Realization dawned.

"She just saw the news. Shit! I need to get in front of this from a PR point of view, I guess." Kade stared out the window, seeing nothing.

"Samantha?" Reece asked.

"Yeah. She'll know how to handle the media. The police already tried to help with a press conference saying it was just vandalism."

"Good. Call Ian and Jillian, they may be able to give some insight..." Reece started.

"I don't want to involve anyone I don't have to. I'm trying to keep this quiet and everything running to the best of my ability here, but I'm not her."

"Yes... I know." Reece sighed.

Kade could hear the chaos in the background on the other end of the phone.

"Dominick?"

"I haven't heard from him since we left Boston. We've got people looking for him. It was like he suddenly disappeared."

"Then FIND him! This is your wheelhouse, Kade. It's time we find this bastard and clean up this mess."

"That's what I'm trying to do!" Kade screamed back into the phone.

"Keep me informed."

Without another word, the phone went dead.

Anger, frustration, agitation, and a sense of being overwhelmed sent Kade over the edge. Slivers of failures to protect in the past pushed against his present. In the next instance, the cell phone went flying across the office and slammed against the wall with a satisfying crack as it bounced to the floor.

"Well," Tanner said as he walked into the room from the command center next door. "I don't know what that phone did to offend you, but I'm glad I'm not your cell phone."

His thick Southern drawl made each word flow like molasses into the next one.

Kade fell into his desk chair and huffed as he watched Tanner walk over and pick up the shattered phone. He tapped his radio and turned toward Kade.

"Folks, we've got a six six six by one. Repeat a six six six by one."

"Really? Please confirm a six six six by one."

Tanner chuckled as he flipped the broken phone through his hand.

"Confirmed."

"Rough day. Wide berth. Copy that."

With that, the radio went silent.

Kade glared at Tanner. It was a good thing they'd been friends for so long or he knew he'd rip into him at this very moment. Matthew Tanner had saved his hide more than once overseas. He swore nothing could rattle the Texas native, but he also knew the amount of demons the man carried.

"What the hell is a six six six by one?" Kade demanded.

"Ah, so you are still with us. I was wondering if that Hulk move meant you'd fallen off the edge. Besides, it's pretty obvious-the person in command just went all beast on a piece of helpless technology."

"Great, a wise guy. Just what I need today." Kade glared at him.

"You're the one who threw the phone just so it would stop ringing. Effective, but you realize it doesn't stop the problem. Right?" Tanner said with a shrug and tossed the phone on the desk in front of him.

Kade picked up the shattered piece of equipment and cringed. He could just hear Alexandra ripping into him for losing his temper and letting things overwhelm him. The military had left him with two important things: the discipline to push through any situation and the scars to give him enough guilt and nightmares to last a lifetime. In this moment, he wasn't sure which one of those things would win the war in the face of his current battles.

"That female detective looked like she's got some bite on her. I knew I should have pushed harder to get audio on these cameras and not just in certain areas." Tanner continued his own thoughts.

"She's not your type," Kade huffed.

"Someone's touchy. Guess you've got a good reason since she walked into your office and took your seat, though I have to admit she looked like a kid in that chair of yours." Tanner grinned.

"Keep it up, Tanner, and the phone won't be the only casualty of the day," Kade growled.

"Will it put you in a better frame of mind if I beat you to a pulp on the sparring mat?" Tanner goaded him.

"I can assure you you'll walk away with a limp."

With that, Tanner laughed. Even Kade knew they were evenly matched, and both would work hard to do any damage to the other.

"Seriously, though, are you going to let the detective help find the bastard who has the entire place on pins and needles? I, for one, am tired of playing by his rules."

"Alexandra would have a conniption if I let the police roam around in here," Kade said with a sigh.

"True, but she's not here. In fact, she's actually on the run from a stalker we can't seem to get close to. We're getting out of our depth here, boss. Don't get me wrong, you've got great people on this one, but we could really use some expensive resources who aren't internally limited."

"The police are rarely limited in their searches," Kade shot back.

"True. But let her help you solve the knife in the door problem. Maybe it will give us enough leads to find out other information along the way. It can't hurt. At this rate, this bastard will run us right into the ground, and Alexandra will never be safe to come home, and that's not really an option. I mean, you can pull off the heels, but they've got to be murder on the feet." Tanner grinned and stuck a toothpick between his teeth.

"Do you just keep those things in your pocket? Every time I see you, there's a toothpick in your mouth."

"It's this or smoke a couple packs a day, and I never liked cigars."

"You don't like cigars? That's blasphemy."

"So when ya going to talk to that pretty detective again?" Tanner pushed.

"When are you going to review the tapes and find out who the hell stuck a knife in our front door?"

"Ah, that's what I was coming in to tell ya when I heard this horrible bang and got all distracted with the phone."

Kade watched the other man shift under his gaze.

"I'll give it to ya straight, we've got nothin'."

"Say again." Kade looked at him, confusion etched across his face.

"We've got nothing. Whoever did this knew the range of the camera, where to put a magnet to knock us out, and covered up too much to get even the most basic facial outline."

He took a deep breath and leveled a glare at Tanner. "You mean to tell me we've got enough cameras around here to capture the sneeze of every high profile person in DC. A twenty-four by seven command center whose staff woke me up after less than three damn hours of sleep, and you can't tell me who put a fucking knife in our front door?" Kade roared.

Tanner took a large step back away from the desk. "That's exactly what I'm telling you, boss."

"You're all fired!" Kade screamed, but Tanner didn't move a muscle. "Did you hear me?"

"I heard the words, and I heard the frustration. I believed the frustration and ignored the words," Tanner said calmly. "When you're ready to listen, we got some information from the footage."

Kade slammed his both fists on his desk and closed his eyes. "Why didn't you start with that?" he boomed.

The constant lack of sleep was wearing on him. He took several deep breaths to find center before he looked back up at Tanner.

"What did you find?" he said with a forced calm.

"The perp was a female. I'd put her at about five foot six or so with long dark hair, though it could be a wig. She was wearing a hoodie and her fingernails were manicured," Tanner stated.

Everything in Kade paused at the report. "A female?"

"Yep. It's confusing us too. She knew exactly where to step to stay out of the line of all but the one edge camera on the porch. That one was taken out by some kind of magnetic device, but her movements were unsure."

For a long second Kade thought about the information.

"Well, this is an unexpected situation," Kade said thoughtfully.

CHAPTER SIX

Jessica stared at her computer. Questions ran through her mind at lightning speed, and not one of them made sense. The end of her pencil bounced in an erratic rhythm on her desk until she threw it toward her screen and stood up to pace.

"What's got you all on edge, Lawson?" Ben Matthews asked.

"There's something about this case that's not sitting right," she replied absently.

"Which case?"

"The knife in the door."

"You mean the knife in the door at the sex club? You're the one that got handed that one? That's a riot. How was the sex club on the inside, anyway?"

"Beautiful. Luxurious. Amazing." She answered without thinking of the consequence.

"Hey, boys, I think our little detective over here liked her outing to our local dungeon."

"Wait. What?"

She spun on her heels and pointedly stared at him.

"You can't tell me you spent time in that place and didn't realize what it was," Ben said with a laugh.

"No. I thought maybe it was a swingers' club or something."

"You mean to tell me you talked to the head of security and walked around the place yet you didn't see any whips and chains?"

"Um, no." She felt the blush creep up her face and was positive every one of them could read her thoughts.

"Oh look, now you've gone and embarrassed her," Jake Malone, one of the beat cops from the scene, said to Ben. "Though to see her work some of those security types over, you'd think she had a whip in her hand."

Jessica groaned. She kept everything about her private life tightlipped and well-guarded. Her previous thoughts of Kade wrapped in her rope surfaced and added fuel to her already radiating skin.

"Lawson." The Captain's voice cut through the bullpen. "My office."

"Looks like someone's pissed off the money boys."

"Give it a rest, Matthews. Mine straps on and makes yours look microscopic," Jessica shot back as she headed for the captain's office. Behind, hoots and hollers followed her. She knew full well if she didn't return the volley and take whatever they dished, she'd forever be an outsider.

Jessica straightened her shoulders and summoned all of her confidence. Their captain was a great man, but there was something about him she found intimidating, but she'd not give him the satisfaction of knowing it any more than the rest of the department.

"Yes, Cap," she said as she stepped through the door.

"Where are you with the Empyrean case?" he asked without looking up from his computer monitor.

"Officially? It's a dead end. We have a mold of a footprint and the knife in the door contained mostly pigs' blood with a trace of human blood. We're running the latter for DNA, but I'm not hopeful at this point. It can easily be ruled vandalism based on what we have in evidence."

"Now tell me what you think, unofficially," he said, leveling his intense gaze directly at her.

"Something's hinky."

"Hinky? Is that an official opinion?"

Jessica shook her head back and forth and looked out the window.

"It's more hunch? Gut feeling? Intuition?" Her explanation came out as questions rather than confident statements, and it irked her.

"So what's this hunch of yours?" he asked and leaned back in his chair. Everything in his movements and actions were done to exude power. Even down to making her stand because her short stature just made her look him in the eye when he was sitting. Reminding her of not only her size but the position in the department. She hated being a probey all over again, but paying dues was always a requirement.

"I think they are hiding something big, at least big to them."

"Explain," he said, leaning forward and resting his large arms on the desk.

"First, why would the owner of the club up and disappear? I talked to the newest member of the security team, and he indicated it wasn't a normal occurrence. Though taking his newness into account, it could be he's misunderstood the situation. But that doesn't explain why the head of security seems so unnerved. It's like he's carrying more than normal. It's not a lack of capability—he seems capable—but like it was foisted upon him." She collected her thoughts.

Normally she'd go for a swim to work out a puzzle, but with her current schedule there was little time for such indulgences, which made her mind race and words tumble forth in a stream of consciousness. She hated being called out when she was still in the middle of the process.

The silence filled the room. Behind his large wooden desk, the captain sat waiting for her to continue.

"And why a knife? Why a bloody knife? And the note- 'If I can't

43

have you, I'll destroy you.' That's not a hoax, that's a threat. We don't know if it is credible, but Mr. Kinkaid knows and he's hiding it. Then there was the reporter at the press conference. He asked about a stalker. None of the interviews on-site brought this piece of information forward. If someone is being stalked, then who and why?"

Jessica let her gaze lose focus as the pieces formed a visual puzzle across her mind. Some of them connected with possibilities while others left more questions.

"Doesn't sound like you're ready to close the case," the captain said with a satisfied smirk.

"But I thought that's what you wanted. A quick close, process it as a vandalism so the money wouldn't scream," Jessica asked, confused.

"You need to learn something fast out here in the civilian world. What we tell the world is a lie, a half truth or done for our own purposes. You did all three in your first press conference," he said with a grin.

"This was a set-up? Throw the probey into the fire and see if she walks or gets scorched? Worse, throw her into a sex club case to see if she squirms?" She seethed but controlled her tone.

"Either you make it or you don't. You knew what this was when I hired you."

Jessica nodded in resignation. She'd fought her entire life for everything she got, and this would be no different.

"What's your next move?" he asked as he turned back to his computer.

"I want to call the reporter who asked about the stalking. Then I dig into the club owner's background before I meet with Mr. Kinkaid to go over the security tapes and see what they found."

The captain nodded. "I think you should attend a couple events there. See how security works, get a read on the members."

"You want me to go to a sex club event?"

"No, I want you to go to the Empyrean Club and see what you find during an event."

"Oh, I'm sure their security will love it."

The captain chuckled. "Kade will hate you being on his turf. He'll see you as a club security risk and a pain in his ass. Either you handle it or deal with what happens."

"Do I have permission to blend into the party in any way necessary?"

"I think that's the only way you'll get anything out of this assignment."

Jessica stifled a grin and attempted to look shocked at his innuendo.

"Now get out of here. I've got work to do," he said with a wave of dismissal.

JESSICA WALKED BACK TO HER DESK IN A CLOUD OF CONFUSION and thought. Nothing was adding up other than the nagging thought that someone was in real trouble, and she didn't like who, based on her hunch.

"I see you survived the captain," Ben started in on her.

"Can it, Matthews! I get the whole women are fragile crap, but if you ever want to go toe to toe on the mat, you'd better bring it because you're going to need it to pick up your bruised ego up when I slam your ass on it," she said, glaring at him.

"Big talk," Ben shot back.

She looked down at her watch.

"How's six this evening sound?"

The entire department got quiet, and suddenly all eyes turned toward them in anticipation.

"I don't fight girls," he mumbled.

"Scared?" she challenged.

Jessica knew she should give him a way out, but if she didn't establish herself, they'd continue to be merciless and think she'd been hired because she was a woman, not because she was up to the task. There was nothing she hated more than being told she'd gotten somewhere because of her size or gender. They didn't have to like her, but they needed to respect her in order for her to get anything done.

"I don't want to hurt you."

She forced a smile. "Maybe I like bruises or is it the fact I like giving them? I always get those two a little confused." She smiled at him. "Come on, big man. You outweigh me by what, almost a hundred and twenty pounds with almost a foot of height. Let's play. Get it out of your system so we can all get back to work."

Nothing in her wanted to fight this man. She abhorred this kind of barbarianism. The whole chest-beating ritual to prove she was less than and needed to be put in her place was annoying, but when the situation called for it, she'd do whatever it took to win.

"Fine," Ben growled. "But if you think I'm going easy on you after this little display, you've got another think coming."

"As long as you can explain my time off to the captain, what do I care? See you at six," she tossed over her shoulder as she headed out of the bullpen.

The entire room lit up in an excited murmur. Everywhere she turned, someone made a comment in her favor or about her demise. She shook her head at the whole spectacle as she made her way to a private phone alcove at the other end of the station.

She pulled her notepad out of her pocket and picked up the phone. With a quick dial of the number, she held her breath.

"Bob Baxter," the voice said on the other end.

"Mr. Baxter, this is Detective Lawson. I was wondering if you had a few minutes. I'd like to ask some questions from the press conference the other morning."

"Is this on the record?"

Jessica smiled at his attempt to get a scoop even in an odd position.

"I'm afraid this is completely off the record. You asked me a question about someone being stalked. Why did you ask that specific question?"

"Ah, it got your attention, did it?"

"Yes. Is there anything to the question or were you fishing in the dark?"

"Both, Detective. There's a rumor going around that the owner of the club's been missing for months. Last time I checked, dominant types in that line of business don't much like being out of control. I mean, what would make someone just disappear?"

"Maybe she's out on business or just needed a break from the whole thing. I don't know. I will guess any business owner needs time off. Maybe she was burnt out?"

"Possibly, but I know you're smarter than that. There's something about the note and the way someone left it," he said conspiratorially. "I smell a significant story here."

"So your question was an observation and conjecture?" she pressed.

"Mostly. There's something going on behind the scenes. I mean, she was involved in the huge scandal with Elizabeth Davies' brother a couple of months ago. They caught Reece Gabriel in photos getting out of the club Dominatrix's car."

"Interesting," she said, scribbling furiously on her notepad.

"Are you sure you won't give me an exclusive on the record interview for this case?" Bob pressed.

"Sorry, Bob. Like I told everyone the other day, based on our analysis, the whole thing is a hoax. I'm sure there's a reasonable explanation for everything else."

"Yeah, in DC they call it a coverup. A word you should put in your vocabulary."

"Noted. Thanks for your time."

"Remember me when you've got something juicy, Detective. You know the media can be your best friend and your worst enemy."

"I'm well aware, but thanks for the warning."

With that, she clicked off the call and stared down at her notes. This day was getting more complicated by the minute.

Jessica rubbed her throbbing temples. The ache in her shoulder screamed in tight agony. For the last few hours she'd stared at the computer monitor, scrolling through every possible piece of information she could dig up about the club owner, Alexandra. Each trail led to one dead end after another, and she thought the whole trail was a bust, except for the fact two names kept catching her attention in the searches. An Atlas Devereaux, the public relations manager for the club, and an Edmund Hurter, a near business genius who also happened to be a member of the club. There was nothing on either of them which would normally make them stand out among the hundreds of club member. No, the only thing which bothered her on an intuitive level was the fact that both of them were currently out of town 'on business.' This meant either they were lovers and off on a long holiday because the club owner didn't need her PR manager's services or she was missing something important.

Her left hand ran along her neck, and she could hear the fit her massage therapist would once again pitch. Every muscle from her mid-back up had knots with knots on them. It's where she carried her stress, but there was little time between cases and life to keep the knots at bay.

The vibration of her phone made her jerk in surprise as the alarm rang out in the now quiet bullpen. Jessica looked around, but the normally bustling bullpen was empty. With a deep breath, she slid her finger across the screen on her phone to silence the light tinkling sound. Under her finger, the screen announced the time to be five forty-five.

She chuckled to herself.

They must be really bored in this place, she thought, standing up from her desk and stretching her tight body. *Better give them a good show then.*

With one final look at the computer screen, she jotted down a name and address, then turned off the computer. Jessica gathered up her notes and shoved them into her bag. Hoisting it onto her shoulder, she looked down at her suit and hoped it wouldn't be too tattered after the upcoming match since she'd not packed any sparring clothes. One day her mouth was going to write a check her body couldn't cash, and she was just hoping today was not that day.

Jessica turned and walked toward the onsite gym. The soft click of her heels echoed off walls like the last march to an execution. A few feet from the gym door, the mumble of excited voices was undeniable, and she knew the entire department had come to watch the spectacle.

With one last deep breath to calm her nerves, she heaved open the gym door. The rousing noise fell completely silent as all eyes turned to her. Like the entrance of a gladiator, she knew the next few minutes would either please the crowd or seal her fate. The crowd parted and created a path straight to the sparring ring. In the center, Ben Matthews stopped stretching and glared at her.

Calmly, she walked to the edge of the ring and set her bag down outside the edge of the mat. Jessica slipped out of her heels and dropped another two inches. The floor felt cool against her flushed skin. Without taking her eyes off her opponent, she shrugged her jacket from her shoulders and folded it. Pulling her shoulder harness off, she placed it on top of the jacket and laid the bundle on her shoes.

"Why aren't you changed?" Ben snarled. "I thought you wanted to fight."

"I wanted no such thing; however, you pushed us into this situation with your chest beating. So here I am, ready to finish this so I can get on with my evening."

Each word was meant to goad him, and based on his expression, she'd landed her mark.

"You can't fight in that," he said, pointing to her.

"Sure I can. Last time I checked, perps don't let me stop and change clothes just because they want to fight. How is this any different?"

"I thought you wanted to spar."

"You mean you think you're going to kick my ass and you don't want me using the excuse that my clothes were inappropriate for the match when you do," she corrected.

49

Ben murmured something incomprehensible.

"Shall we?" Jessica said, motioning to the mat.

Ben nodded.

"Anything off limits, or is this a no-holds-barred, out on the street situation?" she asked with a calm she didn't feel.

"No biting, no spitting," Ben replied, his nostrils flaring in agitation.

"Okay. No biting, no spitting. Anything else off limits?"

"The loser can't whine or sulk."

"Fair," Jessica said with a nod. "How do we define a winner?"

Ben's face screwed up in thought.

"The one who is still conscious," he snarled and then smiled menacingly.

CHAPTER SEVEN

"Hello, big boy," Samantha purred as she walked into the room. "Unless you've got a great piece of PR, a way to stop this stalking business, or you've decided to take the helm of this club, get out," Kade growled without lifting his head from the papers on his desk.

"Oof. Someone's cranky. Maybe a bit of play would help your sullen mood," she replied on her way to pour herself a drink.

He watched her out of the corner of his eye as she moved around the room. Unlike Jessica, she didn't take up space or have an air about her. It wasn't a lack of confidence, but it was different. Jessica was hard and firm on the outside. It didn't matter that she was a foot shorter than him, there was something about her which lit up the room.

"I've got neither the time nor the inclination for play of any sort right now. In case you've not been paying attention, there's a crisis going on around here."

The lead broke off the end of his pencil, and he wanted to throw it across the room. Instead, he restrained the urge and looked up to watch Samantha.

"All work and no play make Kade horrible to deal with," she said as she sat down on the sofa.

Kade pushed away from his desk, grabbed his bottle of water, and walked to his normal seat across from Samantha. Images of Jessica in his chair flooded his mind. Her small frame had been engulfed by it, yet she still looked regal and street tough all at the same time.

"I'll play when this mess is over. Now, please tell me you can at least do the PR lift on this latest issue."

Samantha's face screwed up in irritation. "Dare you doubt me, Mr. Kinkaid?"

"Careful," he warned.

"Ah, yes. I'd apologize, but it was rather appropriate this time."

He said nothing in reply, staring at her until she continued.

"I've reached out to several news agencies to get any information they've dug up. Like we suspected, it's all speculative other than the anonymous tip. The location sensationalized the story, but you already knew that."

She gave him a chance to ask questions, but when he didn't respond she continued with a huff. "I've heard the detective's been digging around through quite a number of backgrounds. You need to make sure she's on our team. Besides, she's really hot. Do you know if she's into all this?"

"Down girl," Kade said with a shake of his head. "She's a police detective on a case. You know mixing business with pleasure would be a mess."

"Or you'd be all over it," Samantha said with a chuckle.

"Neither here nor there. These are the circumstances we are in."

"You know, I liked you so much better when you weren't this sullen."

"I like me much better when one of my best friends and protectees wasn't being stalked by a megalomaniac with more money than a small country, the fate of a business I don't even know how to run wasn't sitting on my shoulders, and I didn't worry about the lives of everyone walking through the front door."

"You mean it used to be easier when the worst issue you faced were paparazzi trying to cause a scandal or someone being stupid in one of the play rooms," Samantha replied.

Kade nodded.

"You've got to find a release, Kade. Even Alexandra had a release valve when all those masks got to her."

He took a long sip of water and let the memories rush over him.

"It's not quite that simple for someone in my position. No one can question my authority even if hitting my knees for a woman were in the cards. Right now I am the face of this club."

"And that is scary with a mug like yours." Samantha grinned.

Kade chuckled. "Looked in the mirror lately?"

"Ouch," she said as she pulled out a compact and dramatically powdered her nose. "At least you still have a sense of humor. I was beginning to worry it was too late for you."

"It takes far more than this 'little' thing to kill me off. Besides, someone's got to keep your ass in line or this place will be in shambles when Alexandra gets back."

"I'm not that bad!"

"We'll agree to disagree. Sounds like you've got everything on your end well in hand."

"I've got a lot of support through all of this. I'm lucky to have so many partners supporting me," Samantha said.

"It takes a village," Kade replied with a grin.

A soft knock on the door interrupted them.

"Mr. Kinkaid, a Detective Lawson is here to see you," Katie, Alexandra's assistant, said from the door. He was more than thankful for her help in keeping everything afloat, but he still found her presence and announcements unnerving.

"Please send her in," he replied and stood to turn to the door.

Jessica limped through the door. A large bruise was blossoming across her cheek and her left eye was swollen.

Everything in Kade ran cold. All he wanted to do was protect her. Take care of her and then wipe out the person who'd dared lay a finger on her. He started toward her but stopped when she held up a hand.

"Don't say a word," she warned.

"Jessica, are you okay? Is there anything I can get you?" he asked, his voice laced with an edge.

With her one good eye, she glared at him, and he fell silent.

Samantha stepped around him in a breezy move and walked over to Jessica.

"I'm Samantha, the club's PR person," she said, sticking out her hand.

The two shook, but the tension in Jessica's frame didn't ease.

"The club's PR person? I thought an Atlas Devereaux was the club's PR manager," she asked with suspicion.

"She is, but she's out of town on business. We're partners at the PR firm McKenzie-Kingston here on the grounds."

"How long has Ms. Devereaux been away on business?" Jessica probed.

"A few months now. She and Alexandra are exploring other business opportunities for expansion," Samantha answered smoothly, but Kade noticed the tension forming in her shoulders.

"Expansion for the club or the PR business?"

"The club's base company, I think. Do you mind if I asked what happened?" Samantha replied to change the conversation.

"I got in a tiff with someone."

"Quite the tiff. Who won?"

"I don't think fighting ever gives a winner or loser," she said, moving her hand over her own body as if to demonstrate her point. "But suffice to say, I took his breath away."

"Okay. On that note, I will exit stage right and get out of the way. I'm sure you've got quite a bit to fill Mr. Kinkaid in on with the case and all. It was nice meeting you, Detective," Samantha said in a rush on her way out the door.

Before anyone could form a reply, she was gone.

"Is she always like that?" Jessica asked.

"Samantha is an acquired taste. Mostly harmless with exceptional skills in many areas, but it takes quite a few people to keep her together," Kade said with a smile. "But I know you didn't come all the way down here to discuss the staff."

Kade stepped out of the conversation area and motioned for her to sit while he walked across the office to his desk. He pulled the second desk drawer open to reveal a well-stocked first aid kit.

Jessica settled into the large chair with slow, stiff movements. It was a familiar move. More than once he'd done the same carefully choreographed dance to sit down after a bar fight and one too many drinks.

Grabbing a pack of pain medicine, two ice packs, and a bandage, he walked back toward the conversation area and picked up a bottle of water on the way. As he sat down on the seat across from Jessica, he twisted one of the chemical ice packs until it gave a resounding pop and handed it to her.

"I'm not your ward, charge, or protectee, Mr. Kinkaid. I am more than capable of taking care of myself."

"Detective, of that I have no doubt; however, you're on my turf and thus my concern until you leave," he challenged, shoving the ice pack toward her.

Jessica rolled her eyes, but the effect was cut in half due to significant swelling. Kade wanted to laugh but thought better of it.

"Here's a bottle of water. Since this club caters to pain, you can choose to partake of the pain medicine or leave it to nature. Whatever makes you happy," he said with a smirk and set the package of pills next to the water bottle.

He watched her flinch when she placed the ice pack against her face. Everything in him wanted to take away her pain, but she wasn't the first fiercely stubborn woman he'd met. The best course of action was to provide the way out of the pain and wait to see what else she needed.

Jessica picked up the pill pack and handed it to him. The small gesture spoke volumes, but Kade knew better than to read into it. For a few minutes the outside world was easier, and everything in him grew quiet.

With ease, he ripped open the pill back, poured the two pills into his hand, and reached it back out to her. When she'd downed the pain medicine, she settled back in the chair. Even in her disheveled state, she was beautiful.

"If you'll allow me, I can stabilize that ankle. I'm banking you've sprained it," he said and held up the bandage. "And in case you really want to argue, it'll just be easier if you let me take care of it."

He watched her shoulders fall. Exhaustion was written all over her body. With the slightest nod, she acquiesced.

Kade smiled. He rose from the couch and pushed the coffee table out of the way. Grabbing the sides of the large chair, he pulled it toward him and leaned over her small form. She smelled like home. Everything about her called to him. His body stirred unbidden, and he bit back a groan.

"I am quite capable of taking care of myself, Mr. Kinkaid," she whispered as she stared up into his eyes with an intensity that matched his own.

"You've made that abundantly clear, Detective."

Their faces hovered inches apart. Neither one moved as their breaths exchanged in their closeness.

He watched her hand wrap around his tie. Everything in him wanted to lean forward and devour her swollen lips, but years of training and self-discipline had him waiting for her next move.

"Well," Jessica said hoarsely, "this is a pleasant surprise."

"What?" Kade asked with genuine confusion.

"You are inches from me. My hand is entangled in your tie. From the response of your body, you want to move forward, and yet you hold steady inches away."

Kade smiled. "Not everything is what it seems inside these walls," he replied cryptically.

She pulled on his tie, bringing him closer. Her lips brushed against his, and he let her take the lead, not wanting to ruin the moment. Jessica pulled harder on the tie. The unexpected move off-balanced him, and he braced harder against the chair so as not to land on top of her.

He let his touch lick gently across her bruised lips. She opened them and stroked his tongue with her own in a gentle kiss. A moment later, Jessica met him with a hungry kiss. Other than her fingers on his tie, her body didn't move. She controlled the depth with the pull and release of pressure on the small fabric around his neck.

Everything else disappeared. He gave over to her demands as their kiss deepened. A low groan escaped from his throat. His cock throbbed with need, but he refused to move unless Jessica pulled him toward her.

The kiss moved back to a soft, gentle caress. Images of her soft lips moving painstakingly slowly across his body danced in his head. Kade pushed past the fact they were supposed to only be working on the current case. He wanted to grab her and feel every inch of her body. To slip his aching cock into her until they were both satiated and satisfied.

Every fantasy he'd ever had seemed to materialize in front of him Keeping still challenged him in ways he'd not experienced since his first heady days in the scene. The sweet torture of her soft caress moving to a demanding kiss and back again scrambled his rational thoughts.

When he didn't think he could take another second, she pushed on his chest, and he stood up. Kade looked down at her small frame. Her face was flushed and there was a hint of satisfaction for a long moment before she shuttered it.

The realization of their situation seemed to hit her hard and fast. Jessica adjusted in the chair and pulled on her jacket to straighten it.

"Well," she said breathlessly, "that was unexpected."

Kade stepped back. He wanted to adjust his painful erection but only shifted slightly as he took his position back on the couch.

Without a word, he picked up the bandage off the table and held it up. Jessica nodded her acceptance. Kade kept his movements gentle and unhurried as he lifted her foot and set it on his leg. He pulled on the shoe and Jessica winced in pain. Her ankle was swollen to the size of a small grapefruit.

"I want to see if it's more than sprained. This will hurt," he said with confidence but hated the look of pain in her eyes.

Jessica grit her teeth as he moved her ankle and foot to different angles. Periodically he heard a hiss of breath or felt her leg tense against him. When he was satisfied it was only a bad sprain, he wrapped the bandage in place.

Kade picked up the other ice pack and twisted it until it gave a satisfying pop. With her foot still resting in his lap, he placed the ice pack against her ankle.

"Now that we have you sorted"—he nodded toward her ankle —"what brings you to this fine establishment this evening, Detective?"

CHAPTER EIGHT

Jessica stared at Kade. Her mind was spinning. How could he move so easily from their kiss back to business? And what was up with this big man caretaking act? She worked to keep her dispassionate outward composure, but her body was a racing mix of arousal and pain. It was a heady combination.

She ran her hands down her pants to calm her frayed nerves and inhaled deeply to regain her own control. His eyes never wavered from her like he was taking in the most minute information.

"How long has the club owner been away?"

Kade's reaction told her she'd hit a nerve. *Two can play at the observation game, big boy*, she thought to herself. He shifted uncomfortably on the couch but not enough to jostle her ankle still lying across his leg.

"A few weeks," he replied.

"Define a few," Jessica pushed. She wanted answers. Something wasn't adding up in this situation.

"A small number, a handful, not many, hardly any, more than one," Kade said with a smirk.

Jessica pinched the bridge of her nose. The strain of the day was wearing on her, and she wasn't up to this game play. A wave of exhaustion hit, and she closed her eyes and tried to refocus on the best way to get Kade to give her more information on what was going on around here.

"Maybe we should take this up tomorrow, Detective," he mumbled.

She shook her head and forced her eyelids back open. The coolness of the ice pack on her cheek worked through the bruise she knew was forming, and her body screamed for rest.

"If you'll just tell me what I need to know, then I can be on my way," she tossed back.

"With all due respect, you are in no shape to drive, and this conversation would be best when you are well rested."

His tone told her he would not budge, and she was tired of fighting for her own position today. "Mr. Kinkaid, I can take care of myself. The faster you tell me what is happening here, the faster I'll be out of your hair." Her words slurred slightly, and she pushed against the chair to sit up straighter. The move jostled her ankle, and she winced as pain ignited through her leg.

"Obviously," he said dryly.

"Are you always this stubborn?"

"Yes. Especially when it comes to making sure the people around me are well taken care of."

"I'm not one of 'your people,' Mr. Kinkaid," she said as her eyes drifted closed again. Jessica fought against her traitorous body, but the need to tap out pulled on her like a heavy blanket across her senses.

"You are under my roof, so to speak. So for the moment, you are part of 'my people.'"

His deep voice soothed across her senses. *Just for a minute*, she thought. *I can close my eyes for just a minute.*

Darkness drifted across her senses as sleep demanded its due. In her dreams, strong arms cradled her body against a broad warm chest. She let out a soft moan as her body melted into his. The man in her dream carried her through the maze of a castle, up and downstairs and through breezy passages until he carefully lay her upon a gloriously soft bed. With a soft kiss to her forehead, the world faded away.

———

THE SMELL OF BACON MIXED WITH COFFEE URGED JESSICA TO wakefulness. She sighed with contentment until pain seared through her body. Jessica's eyes shot open, and she scrambled for the gun under her pillow. When it wasn't there, panic rose, and she sat straight up. The bedroom was beautifully decorated with a modern minimalist style, leaving much of it open and airy.

She looked down and realized she was still in her now very rumpled suit. Pain streaked through her ankle at her sudden movements, and she groaned when the rest of her body followed its lead. Everything in her told her she'd better have gotten the license plate of the truck that took her out because it was the only explanation for feeling this poorly and not remembering drinking too much.

Sounds from the other room drew her attention, and she focused on the words. She needed to assess her situation, locate her gun, and figure out where the hell she was right now.

"Is she awake yet?" a distant male voice asked with a tone of amusement.

"Not yet. She went through quite a beating. Her eye was almost swollen shut last night, and somehow she sprained her left ankle, but I don't think it was that bad. She was walking on it when she came into the club. A couple of days of rest and stability and it should be good again."

"You know she will want to kill you because you did the whole damsel in distress and whisked her away to your lair," the distant male replied.

"She's no damsel in distress, I assure you. And it's not my lair. I borrowed the apartment because it was close. She fell asleep in the chair for Christ's sake. What was I supposed to do? Put her in a car and risk killing herself or someone else because she fell asleep behind the wheel?"

There was a long silence.

"That was one hell of a kiss by the way," the distant man said, the smirk evident in his voice.

"Tanner, unless you have business to report, I have better things to do with my morning," Kade replied.

Jessica flushed at the mention of the kiss. The memories of the previous evening came flooding back in a rush. What had she done? She was investigating a crime, and she'd kissed someone who was part of the investigation. She pinched the bridge of her nose as her mind berated her for the illogical actions.

In response, her body told her how amazing it was to have a man hover right out of reach because she'd willed it with the smallest motion. The heady combination of power and lust that filled the moment brought her body to an almost uncontrollable need in seconds.

The internal war frustrated her. On one hand, she'd just crossed a professional boundary, and everything in her should feel shame, but she didn't. Everything in her wanted him. She knew the situation could go no further, but it would make for some amazing fantasies as she imagined all the places she wanted to feel his amazing tongue on her body.

"Good morning." Kade's deep voice broke through her conflicting thoughts.

"Good morning. Where the hell am I?"

Kade chuckled. "Ah, still feisty as ever, even when someone tries to save your life."

"I didn't think my life was in danger under your roof," she countered.

"Which is why you are still here," he said, ending the conversation. "I've had clothes brought up for you, as I'm sure you don't want to go through the day in the same suit you slept in. Through those doors is a well-appointed bath. I'm sure you'll find everything you'll need. When you are ready, there is breakfast on the kitchen island."

"Thank you," Jessica said, in awe of his efficiency.

"Glad to be of service," he said with a slight nod and pivoted to exit the room.

Jessica sat for a long minute staring at the door and wondering what world she'd just fallen into because she'd never encountered a man like Kade before.

She hobbled into the bathroom. Large thick towels sat in perfect alignment on a shelf. The shower to her right was big enough to accommodate at least three people, and everything she needed from a toothbrush to small bottles of makeup lay out across the vanity. It reminded her of a resort experience, not a place she'd crashed because she'd made a bad decision to keep working after her spar with Ben Matthews rather than going home like a sane person.

Jessica moved near the shower.

"Please state temperature," a male voice rang out in the bathroom.

With a startle, she yelped as she slammed her foot onto the tile to keep her balance. Her sprained ankle didn't support her weight, and she groaned as she grabbed for the vanity top. When the throbbing eased, she looked around and re-approached the shower.

"Please state temperature," it said again.

"One hundred and two degrees," Jessica replied tentatively.

"One hundred and two degrees Fahrenheit confirmed," the voice answered. As soon as the sentence was complete, the shower automatically started, and Jessica stared at it in wonder and amusement.

Carefully she stripped out of her clothes, unwrapped her ankle, and stepped under the steaming water. Her muscles immediately clenched under the water's onslaught. Every cut and bruise seared through her skin, and she moaned in both pleasure and pain but in all the wrong proportions.

What was she thinking to take on a guy the size of Ben Matthews? She berated herself with each new twinge. It would have just been smarter to walk away. Instead, she fell right into his chest-pounding ego fight. She might have won by getting in a solid combination of moves during what could only be described as a brawl, but it came with a high cost. There was no way she would show her face in the office with one eye swollen shut and a face with every shade of purple and yellow to remind everyone he'd gotten the best of her more than once.

She was tired of the constant need to prove herself in a man's world. From the military to police work, every time she started over there was always at least one Neanderthal who wanted to prove the male myths were true. At five foot five, she was already a target. They always wanted to drive home the idea they thought she wasn't strong enough, smart enough, too soft, too scared, or any of the thousands of mantras of the *men are beasts and women should stay home to make babies* crowd.

Even with almost a foot and a hundred pounds on her, she'd taken him down and brought him to unconsciousness with a choke hold from her knee. It was the price of constantly proving her right to be on the front lines with the men rather than being respected for her position. She'd won, but winning and walking away unscathed were two vastly different things.

Jessica stepped out of the shower and proceeded to gingerly dry off. Taking time to put on makeup and fix her hair wasn't a luxury she was accustomed to enjoying. She brushed her teeth as she read through the assortment of makeup. It was impressive in addressing her current problems, and she wondered at who would have thought of things like bruise cover or a concealer to cover the redness from the scratches on her face.

Thirty minutes later, she was satisfied that she looked somewhat presentable. It was a tall order when one eye was still mostly swollen shut, but at least it was better. Wrapping the last part of the bandage around her foot, she hobbled to the kitchen and braced herself to face Kade. With each step, the memories from the night before flooded to the forefront of her mind, and she groaned. Better to set the record straight about the mistake she'd made with that kiss before everything got out of hand.

CHAPTER NINE

"Good morning, Detective," Kade said from the other side of the large kitchen island. "I hope you slept well."

The aubergine pantsuit fit her curves much better than the boxy one she'd worn the day before. She moved across the room with a stiff grace. It was obvious her body ached, but she refused to give in to the pain.

Once she'd reached the island, he watched as she picked up a coffee mug. Pouring the rich, hot black liquid into it, she held up a hand for him to stop when he started to speak and pointed to the mug. After she took several long sips, she looked up with a nod as if to release him.

Kade chuckled and slid a packet of Ibuprofen toward her.

Jessica tore it open and downed the two pills easily, then returned to focus on her coffee. When she picked up the pot to refill the mug, he tried again.

"There is bacon, bagels, hash browns, and I can cook you eggs in any style you wish. As I did not have an opportunity to ask if you had any allergies or preferences, I put on a basic spread. If you do, please let me know. This is a well-stocked kitchen, and I can cater to any of your needs," Kade said smoothly as he watched her reaction.

She looked at him over her coffee mug with confusion.

"Your captain called this morning to tell me he wanted you to attend the event this weekend. I advised him you needed to work from here for the week to prepare. It would give you an opportunity to understand the grounds layout, choose how you would like to present yourself, and heal. And before you ask, no, I didn't tell him that last part."

Jessica raised an eyebrow in his direction. He shifted slightly but refused to move under her intense gaze. There was something about this woman that intrigued him. He'd known women who wanted to go toe to toe with men, but they often tipped the scale and lost the soft femininity he craved.

He saw none of it as a weakness but rather a gift to be treasured. Something about her drew his attention even when logic demanded he didn't have time for such a distraction.

"Are you always this accommodating to your guests, Mr. Kinkaid?"

The question startled him, and a long silence hung in the air.

"I don't understand what you are asking, Detective."

"Do you often bring women to your apartment and fix them breakfast the next morning?"

"Let me correct a few things before things get out of hand. First, this is Atlas' apartment. It is her secondary residence when the club or one of her clients needs her to work a large project. Second, I don't cook for just anyone, and breakfast isn't really a stretch."

"To clarify, you've brought me into another woman's apartment, let me sleep in her bed, and used her food to cook me breakfast."

"You make it sound far more torrid than it is, Detective." Kade smiled.

"Where did you sleep last night?"

"On the couch. I knew you might wake up in pain or disoriented this morning, and I wanted to be close in case you needed anything."

"Where's my gun?" she asked flatly.

"In the safe. I wasn't sure where you kept it, but I guessed it was normally under your pillow, and I didn't want to get accidentally shot if you woke up startled," he answered matter-of-factly.

"Good call. I reached for it this morning."

He nodded as if he understood.

"Where do you keep yours?" Jessica asked.

"I used to keep it under my pillow," he replied.

Kade suppressed the memories, but the shudder still ran through him.

"Based on that answer, I presume there is a reason you've moved it."

"Yes. It's a long story and thankfully has nothing to do with it being under my pillow," he stated without elaborating further.

"PTSD?"

He nodded. "Now what would you like for breakfast, Detective?"

"Bacon, eggs sunny side up, hash browns, and a glass of orange juice."

"I love a woman who knows exactly what she wants." He grinned at her and moved about the kitchen to fulfill her request. "Orange juice with or without pulp?"

"Either is fine."

Kade turned, grabbed the orange juice, and poured her a large glass.

She watched the pulp dance and swirl in the eddies of the liquid.

"What if I'd said no pulp?" she asked suddenly.

He looked up at her and it was his turn to allow confusion to mar his face.

"Then I would have strained it," Kade stated as if it were the most normal answer.

"Seriously?" Jessica asked in shock.

"Of course. Why would one not be prepared to provide what they've offered? Or what would please someone else?"

He watched her shake her head and wished for the thousandth time since meeting her he could read her thoughts. The woman was an enigma, and he would enjoy figuring her out.

He set the plate in front of her. A look of sheer joy rippled across her face when she bit into the bacon. Picking up her fork, she cut around the whites of the eggs, leaving the liquid yokes. Kade watched in fascination as she dissected her breakfast.

"Aren't you going to eat?" she asked when she looked up and found him watching her.

"I ate breakfast after my run this morning," Kade stated.

"You don't have to babysit me. I'll get out of your hair so you can get to work," she said with an uncomfortable shift in her seat.

"Detective, let's get a few things clear. I wasn't joking about the conversation with your captain. If you're going to attend an event here this weekend, you'll need the week to prepare. We need to get you a membership to the club, teach you the layout of the main house and the grounds, get the appropriate clothes, and pamper you in the spa. No offense, but your rough and tumble look won't fly with the membership here. Either you look the part or you give up finding whatever it is you think is here," Kade said.

There was no question in his tone. Each statement was a fact.

"And how do you think I fit into this world of yours, Mr. Kinkaid?" she snapped.

"That, Detective, is a question only you can answer."

The door to the apartment entrance chimed, and Kade hit the button on the tablet lying beside his hand to show the security camera. Samantha's smirking face popped up, and he hit the button to release the front door locks.

A minute later, Samantha bounded up the stairs.

"Oh Kade, you shouldn't have," she crooned as she eyed the breakfast spread on the kitchen island.

"I didn't," Kade mumbled as he watched Samantha pour herself a cup of coffee. Across the island, Jessica watched the exchange with rapt attention, and he shook his head.

"Good morning, Detective," Samantha said in between bites of bacon. "I hope you slept well."

"Good morning, Samantha. I did, thank you," Jessica replied with a clipped formality.

"Since you're here, I need your help," Kade said as he turned toward Samantha.

"Do I even want to know?"

"It involves shopping with Alexandra's expense account," he said dryly.

"I'm in," she answered without hesitation.

"You don't even know what I want you to do."

"It involves Alexandra's expense account, and that's all I usually need to know."

Kade watched Jessica raise an eyebrow, but she didn't interject.

"There's more to it than spending the boss' money," Kade said with authority.

"You always know how to ruin a good time with a catch to a great deal."

"I need you to bring the detective up to speed on the club. My schedule is full today trying to get all the preparations complete, besides my normal duties. She must understand the rules, go through the membership protocols, be groomed and dressed appropriately."

"You know, the rest of us juggle multiple jobs on a normal basis," Samantha countered.

"Yes, and if you fail there's generally a way to recover. If I fail, someone might end up hurt or dead—again."

The words slipped out before he could stop them, and he watched Jessica's head spin in his direction. He needed to get out of here before he said something stupid.

"Fine," Samantha replied, feigning distress. "I'll make sure to spend time at the spa, buy new clothes, and tell Jessica all your secrets."

Kade glared at her, but she only returned a Cheshire grin.

"Don't believe a word she says, Detective. Except about the club, that's probably the safest subject with this one," he said, hiking his thumb toward Samantha and smiling.

He turned and shot a warning look at his friend. "I'll be in my office if you need me."

With that, he turned and hustled down the apartment's front stairs.

Kade walked through the receptionist's office of the PR firm and reached for the door at the exact moment it opened. With a quick reverse, he stepped back to prevent getting hit. He expected to see Melodie, the PR firm's receptionist, making her way into the office. Instead, Cassandra walked in, looking nervous.

"Good morning, Cassandra. What brings you to McKenzie-Kingston this early in the morning?" Kade asked with suspicion.

Cassandra jumped back with a start. "Um... good morning, Kade," she said nervously.

"Is there something you need?"

"I was looking for Samantha or Melodie."

"Why?"

"Well, I was working through, uh, the books Alexandra recommended. And, well, I thought... um, maybe Samantha would be able to, um, well... give me a perspective."

Kade raised an eyebrow.

"Let me get this straight. You're breaking a cardinal rule of separation by coming to Ms. Kingston's workplace to ask her a question about things which happen in the club?"

"When you put it that way..." she said, her eyes hitting the ground and her hand moving behind her back.

"And if you were coming to talk to Samantha, why were you looking for Melodie?"

"I thought she might help me find her or get an appointment on her calendar."

"You would pay for your appointment time at the PR firm?"

Cassandra looked up at him shocked, as if what he said was the most unreasonable thing she'd ever heard.

"It was just questions. Why would I pay her for information easily found on the internet?"

"If that's the case, why don't you go look them up and return it in a ten-page research paper?" he challenged.

"I don't owe you anything. You aren't Alexandra."

"This much is true. I don't look that damn good in a dress. However, until she returns from her business trip, her authority is in my hands and carries the same weight."

"Maybe someone should put you in your little submissive place, Kade. It seems you're getting too big for your position."

Kade took two steps forward, stepping into Cassandra's personal space. Even at five foot seven inches, she still had to look up to see him.

"Let's get something straight right here and right now. It doesn't matter which side of the dynamics I choose around here, I am still in charge. When Alexandra is here, my authority is my own. When she is not here, my authority is hers combined with my own. If you think you are up to the task, then you are either stupid or arrogant. Never make the mistake that a submissive is weak because they submit, or that they can take a position of leadership, as you've see throughout our mentorship. Just because you observe me in a submissive position to someone else doesn't mean I'm submissive in any way to you. Do we have an understanding?"

Cassandra nodded and took several steps back until she bounced against the front door.

"New topic for your research paper. Ten reasons people submit and why it isn't a weakness," Kade said but didn't move toward her.

"I don't owe you anything," she said with a glare.

"Let me put it in simpler terms. You are here by the grace of Alexandra on a provisional membership based on a guest pass. Alexandra extended a provisional membership to you prior to leaving on unexpected business based on you following through on the in-house mentorship program. Since I have neglected your program because of multiple factors, I'm prioritizing my interest in your education. You can either do as I ask or I can revoke your membership," Kade said casually.

"You can't do that," Cassandra screeched.

"Can. And will."

He watched Cassandra's face fill with rage and waited for the explosion.

"Fine," she spat.

"Paper is due Thursday end of business. That is standard business. As in five o'clock post meridian. If it isn't up to my standards, not only will you not attend the event this weekend, but I will immediately revoke your membership. You can appeal the decision upon Alexandra's return."

"And when will that be?" she said with too much interest.

"When she returns."

"She'll be hearing about this upon her return," Cassandra sneered.

Kade chuckled. "You can bank on it," he said.

He leaned against the wall and endured her petulant staring contest for the next few minutes until she gave up and wrenched the door open. Without grace, she stormed out of the PR firm and back toward the club.

Kade ran a hand through his hair and exhaled. Something about the encounter wasn't sitting right with him. While they had limited his interactions, Cassandra has always been cordial until now. He made a mental note to follow up on it later, but he knew there was a stack of work already piling up on his desk. Alexandra owed him after this one, he thought as he made his way back to the club's security office.

CHAPTER TEN

"**D**are I ask what happened to you yesterday?" Samantha asked between bites of bacon.

"Are you always this direct?"

Samantha laughed and took a sip of her coffee.

"I find it facilitates getting to the core of issues, finding out what people value most and hide. I'd blame it on New Jersey or maybe it's my combination of partners. Regardless, it works-most of the time," she said matter-of-factly.

"Did you say partners, as in plural?"

Samantha nodded but didn't elaborate. She spun the tablet Kade had used around and punched in a couple of combinations.

"Looks like you've got quite a full schedule this week. Kade extended a provisional membership to you..." Samantha said without a pause and wrinkled her brow.

"What's with the look? It's a provisional membership, and I'm here for work," Jessica said.

"No. It's actually a full club membership contingent only on the paperwork, bloodwork, and skills assessment," Samantha said and then smiled.

"It's probably just a mistake, an oversight in trying to make me look more legitimate 'undercover.'"

"Kade doesn't make mistakes like that. If he gave you a full membership, it's on purpose. Only two people can revoke a membership or grant one, and there's only a handful of reasons for revocation."

"Let's be reasonable for a minute. Mr. Kinkaid thought he'd given me a provisional membership, accidentally marked full. Simple paperwork error," Jessica said with a shrug.

"Let me fill you in on something, Detective Lawson. Kade had to override three different warnings against a full membership without you going through the provisional process to make this happen."

Jessica stared at Samantha for a long minute. The weight of the information sat heavy on her shoulders, but she didn't understand its meaning or significance.

Without looking up, Samantha asked, "How did you say you got that bruised eye?"

"A colleague challenged me to spar," Jessica started and pulled up short. "It's inconsequential to the case. You said there was a series of assessments I needed to pass?"

Samantha grinned and nodded.

"Let's finish filling out your membership so it will pull up the appropriate list. How do you identify?"

"Identify? I'm not sure what you're asking."

"Are you a top, bottom, switch, Dominant, submissive-all the above, none of the above?"

The question wasn't surprising, though Jessica rarely said the words out loud. Few people knew of her particular desires. She didn't fit into the commercial image of a 'Dominatrix' or 'Domme' or whatever they wanted to call a female Dominant these days. It was difficult enough being a female Dominant without all of the labels and baggage of social media.

Samantha looked up from the tablet expectantly.

"Dominant," Jessica said simply.

"Perfect."

A slow smile curled around Samantha's lips as she continued to type.

"Particular kinks?"

Jessica took a slow, deep breath. "Straight razors, knives, wax, chastity, and submission. I think that's enough to get the paperwork started," she said dryly.

"A woman who loves sharp things, denies pleasure until she deems it is her wish to grant it, paints with wax, and loves to see a person kneeling before her," Samantha said as she typed, a grin planted firmly on her face. "Are you first aid certified?"

"I am."

"Last blood test?"

"Six months ago."

"How did you learn your skills?"

"A combination of my job, life experiences, and a mentor in the scene, though I hesitate to call him that," Jessica said with disdain.

"Why?" Samantha asked, the grin falling from her face as she looked up from the tablet.

"There are things we learn out of force. It takes time to reconcile it when you realize you enjoy it. Even more when you realize you enjoy doing it to someone else," Jessica answered as she stared across the kitchen as if lost in a memory.

"You and At... Alexandra will get along famously. Both of you hold too much to the chest and think pride is strength. You do realize it cometh before a solid fall, right?"

Jessica nodded. "Oh, I've been made aware of that fact more than once in life. As to holding things close to the vest, I find it keeps things relative and compartmentalized. Removes the... emotions from the equation," she said with a slight hesitation.

"Removes the emotions from the equation? You must be a hoot at parties. The emotions are the equation. The connection and bond in any experience," Samantha said, cocking her head to the side and staring at Jessica.

"You've obviously never worked in a field which required logic and reason to compete on an even footing. You seem like a wonderfully open free spirit who wants everyone to be happy and live their best life."

It was Samantha's turn to stare at Jessica agape. "A profiler?"

"A detective, as you already know. Reading people is part of the job," she said coolly.

"The men here are in so much trouble and they won't even see you coming," Samantha mumbled.

Jessica raised an eyebrow and took a long sip of her coffee.

"We need to get one thing straight. I'm here for the case. If I deem there's nothing here, other than a bout of harassment, then I'm out of here. My proclivities don't come into play except they allow me to blend. I'm already irritated Kade chose to talk to the captain without consulting me and irritated he agreed, though not surprised from our conversation yesterday."

"Kade is... prideful, protective, and possessive. Those traits can make him stubborn, willful, stoic, and unthinking," Samantha offered.

"It makes him a man who stepped all over me because I was stupid, vulnerable, and weak."

"You got one of those things right, but only one. It makes him a man. I've known Kade for a long time, and his heart is in the right place."

Silence lingered between them. Frustration welled in Jessica when she remembered her irrational move and the kiss the night before. He'd been so close and smelled so good. Under him she wasn't intimidated or less. For the first time in far too long, the world lifted from her shoulders, and she could breathe. He gave only what she asked and waited on her to take the next step. Never in her life had she met a man like him. *This is a case*, she reminded herself. Her only focus was finding out what was going on around here. Not fooling around with the locals.

She squared her shoulders and forced a smile. "Where do we start?"

"Let's start with a wardrobe. When's the last time you wore a corset?" Samantha grinned.

"It's been years since I've put one on."

"Good, let's start there."

Outwardly Jessica nodded. Inwardly she cringed as the pain in her ribs lit up again. If she were a betting woman, she'd bank at least two of them were cracked. This was going to be a long week.

Wardrobe was one of the last things on the list. For the past four hours Jessica had finished the paperwork, taken a long tour of the facilities, done a blood draw, threatened Samantha's life if she even thought about the spa, and then landed in a never-ending rotation of outfits.

She breathed a deep sigh of relief when Samantha stepped back to observe her work.

The black brocade waist-cincher completely changed the look of the aubergine business suit. It tucked right under Jessica's bustline, slightly pleating the gray camisole underneath. Looking in the mirror, she admitted there was something alluring about the hidden garment when her jacket was buttoned. The added benefit of support to her ribs didn't go unnoticed as the compression relieved some pain in her ribs.

"Who knew a business suit could look so sexy?" Samantha said to the woman standing next to her.

She hadn't introduced them; instead she'd worked her way through a large closet of clothes, each time declaring the outfit wasn't right in this way or that until Jessica cried uncle when her body refused to deal with all the movement. Finally, she'd settled on exchanging the original white button-down under the suit for a gray camisole and waist-cincher. Her already small waist looked almost impossibly small, and they'd barely cinched it down.

"All of this dress-up has been fun, but I've got work to do," she finally announced.

Samantha's face fell, and she huffed.

"I suppose. At least we've got the necessary measurements and Emily here does wonders with a needle and thread," she said proudly.

"That's great," Jessica replied, half listening. "Do you know where I can find Kade?"

She watched Samantha tap the tablet.

"He's in his office. Let me ping him for you."

Jessica made her way to a chair and gingerly lowered herself down. Everything hurt, but that was the price for being stupid and challenging one of the biggest men in the department. She would never live this one down and only hoped everyone would remember she'd actually won, though he'd walked away in far better shape.

"Kade is meeting with Ian Breckenridge. He's asked that I show you to his office," Samantha said, pulling Jessica out of her thoughts.

"Excellent. It's about time I quit all of this nonsense and get back to work."

"All work and no play," Samantha quipped.

"Makes me a damn good detective," Jessica finished.

"Without a life."

Jessica shrugged and rose from the chair. "I understand you and Alexandra are close, based on your comments and my investigation," she said as they walked out of the room.

"You could say I've known Alexandra all her life."

"So you two grew up together?"

"In a matter of speaking, yes."

She made a note of the cryptic answer and changed tactics.

"You're Atlas Devereaux's business partner? How long have you known her?"

"We went to college together. Atlas lived on campus and I commuted. We happened to meet in the library when she was supposed to be working a grad paper in business and I was looking up a juicy story for a PR research paper. We've been friends and business partners, in some form, ever since."

"How did Atlas and Alexandra meet?"

Samantha looked down at the floor as if she was thinking about the question.

"College. Atlas was the TA for a professor and they formed a deep friendship."

"I'd love to meet Atlas. Do you know when she'll be back?" Jessica pushed. Something wasn't adding up.

"No, Detective, I don't know when either of them will be back. I'm not always privy to the projects of either Atlas or Alexandra," she said with annoyance.

"But you're Atlas' business partner."

"An astute observation. And on that note, this is Kade's office. I'm sure he's more than capable of filling you in on any details you might desire. It's been a pleasure, but I need to get back to the PR firm."

Samantha nodded slightly, turned on her heel, and headed back toward the front of the building in a brisk walk.

She wanted to follow her and get to the bottom of the strange shift in mood, but the door behind her opened and a familiar voice called her.

"Come in, Detective," Kade said. "We were just discussing the situation with the knife."

CHAPTER ELEVEN

K ade watched her straighten her shoulders and turn to face him. The makeup on her cheek was smudging enough to show a hint of the bruise underneath. Its presence made him want to punch someone for hurting her, but he'd learned enough to know voicing such a thought was a mistake. Jessica might be small, but there wasn't anything fragile about her.

She gave him a reserved smile and walked past him into the room. He pivoted and began the introductions as he followed behind her.

"Detective, this is Mr. Ian Breckenridge. He owns Breckenridge Security and contracts with us on the weekend to add to our team. Ian, this is Detective Jessica Lawson," he said, completing the introduction as she reached the seating area.

"A pleasure to meet you, Mr. Breckenridge," Jessica said and reached out her hand.

"You've been quite the topic of conversation, Detective Lawson," Ian said and smiled at her.

"Interesting," she replied and looked over at Kade.

"Ian has some theories about the knife, and I've cued up the security tapes," he said, trying to move her focus away from Ian's comment.

"If that's how you want to play it, Mr. Kinkaid, please proceed, but we're coming back to how I was the topic of conversation."

Ian chuckled and drew her attention. Kade glared at him.

"Payback sucks, my friend," he tossed back at Kade.

He watched Jessica take over his chair, but this time she perched right on the edge of it rather than leaning back. The movements were stiff and careful as she settled, crossing her feet at the ankles. She leaned her body until her weight shifted to her right arm propped on the armrest as her left hand flipped the button of her jacket open. Kade's heart nearly stopped at the sight of the corset peeking out between the sides of her jacket.

"Nice outfit," Ian said as he admired her from across the conversation area.

"You were going to tell me about the situation at hand. There's far more to it than a harassing knife in the door," she continued without acknowledgement.

Ian looked up at him, but Kade had lost most of his communication ability. He knew Ian would tease him mercilessly for it later, but right now he had to get through this meeting.

"Prior to the knife in the door, there were a few incidents on the grounds. A couple of security breaches, a member who overstepped his boundaries and such, but most of them didn't add up too much," Ian started.

"These types of situations aren't run of the mill, but they aren't unusual either," Kade said, catching up with the conversation and sitting down beside Jessica. "Periodic breaches, members pushing boundaries with the staff or other members are part of this business."

"Okay. What changed?"

"Direct, I like that," Ian said and nodded toward Kade.

"The knife escalated the situation," Kade responded to the detective's question.

84

"How has Alexandra handled these escalations at her club?" she asked.

Kade looked at Ian to communicate his concern, but Ian shook his head.

"She's letting her security team handle it because it is our job," he said with finality.

He watched her head jerk up and look at him. It took every ounce of control to sit still under her scrutiny. The intensity of her gaze made him think she could read everything he wasn't saying, but trust was built and earned. While his emotions might scream to tell her everything and ask for help, his head told him there was nothing more dangerous.

"Does your crack security team know why there was a knife in the door?" she asked with a slight drawl.

This time he returned her gaze, challenging her to take control or be part of the team.

"We have a good idea, but we wanted your take on the situation," he said without looking away.

Across the room, Ian cleared his throat and hit the remote to click on the monitor set up on a moveable cart at the other end of the office. A grainy image of the front of the club played out in front of them, then a sudden streak of long hair and a piece of paper fluttered into view. A second or two later, the same fuzzy image passed back in front of the camera. After the video played, a still image of the retreating shape appeared.

"How tall is the front door?" Jessica asked without taking her eyes off the image.

"Seven feet six inches," Kade responded.

"Female, long hair, over five seven but under six feet tall, size nine shoe," she stated with certainty.

Kade stared at her in wonderment.

"Basis of conclusion?" Ian inquired.

"Her hair is well past her shoulder, which doesn't tell us anything. Her build is slight, but there's a curve in her waist, and the police found the footprint of a woman just off the paving stones during the investigation," she said.

"Show-off," Ian quipped.

Jessica smirked.

"Utilization of all resources," she said with a laugh. "Is this the best video you've got? I would have thought with the cost of membership and the type of people walking through those doors, you'd have better surveillance."

"We do," Kade said defensively.

"What he means is there are a number of better quality cameras surveilling the area but someone knocked them out with a magnetic device and others were hacked. Most members can see the large pan and tilt cameras, but there are a couple of places where the cameras are built into the structure and on a different network as a backup," Ian said, throwing Kade a *get it together* look.

"You think this was a professional job?"

"Professional-no. Professional equipment? State-of-the art," Kade said.

"Normally that would be a defining situation, but around here everyone has more money than God," Jessica quipped. "Speaking of, what do you know about Edmund Hurter?"

A knot formed in Kade's stomach. The mention of the one man who'd upended Alexandra's world and as a result, a whole host of other people, was a name he hated to hear. With no proof of wrongdoing, he'd remained a member of the club. Alexandra's secret-keeping did not help the situation and eventually forced her to run because she hadn't trusted him to keep her safe. Not that he'd blame her. He had blood on his hands from not being able to keep a charge safe in the past. This was just another reminder of his failures.

"He's a member here," he stated calmly.

"With all due respect, I'd already ascertained that much. What is his relationship with either Atlas or Alexandra?"

"Why do you ask, Detective?"

This time it was Ian's turn to volley the question. Kade glanced over at his friend, who was now sitting forward on the couch.

"A reporter made a comment about stalking after the press conference, so I did a little digging. Based on general information, Atlas Devereaux has been gone on business for several months, as have Alexandra and Edmund. Now, they could all be in different places in the world, but I have a hard time buying such coincidences. So either they are all partners together and they eloped, two of them are partners and the other one is watching, or someone is following someone around. So gentlemen, which one is it?"

The silence in the room was like a blanket. Kade's mind spun, and he watched Ian shake his head.

"Quite the set of conclusions, Detective," Ian said, breaking the silence and ending the statement with a large exhale.

"According to the FAA, Mr. Hurter's plane took off from Dulles headed to St. Kitts four days ago. I hear it's beautiful. The crystal clear waters, the warm weather..." Jessica said calmly.

"Wait, did you say his plane took off four days ago headed for St. Kitts?" Kade interjected.

"Yes, why?"

"Fuck!"

"I'm on it," Ian said jumping up from the couch and reaching for his phone.

Kade ran an anxious hand through his hair.

"Well, Detective, it looks like you may have just given us the lead we needed and hate," Kade said.

"What the hell is going on here?" Jessica growled.

"Was there an NDA in your welcome package?" Kade asked hastily.

"Yes."

"And you signed it?"

"Yes."

He stood and walked over to his desk. Tapping the spacebar, his monitor lit up under the command and he quickly navigated to the

87

club's intake documentation until he found her paperwork. Thankful for Samantha's efficiency, he flipped through the files until he found the non-disclosure agreement with her signature on it. Then he flipped to her orientation page-Dominant, knives, wax play, chastity, submission. With a stifled moan, he chastised himself and shut down the page.

"Okay, I see it in the system."

"Wonderful," Jessica replied sarcastically.

"I'm juggling knives here, Detective; I don't need a paper cut," Kade shot back.

"Fair. Now tell me about those knives."

Kade took a deep breath and walked back toward her.

"Mr. Hurter was a client of Alexandra's. She'd been his professional Dominant for several years and it seemed to satisfy his needs until the day he proposed to her. When she refused him, he stalked her and threatened everyone around her. She didn't trust me enough to tell me and ran out of fear. We didn't put the pieces together until fairly recently when Ian had a run-in with him at a restaurant. The man is ruthless in his pursuit and wicked smart. Alexandra's been hiding in St. Kitts with Reece Gabriel. If he's found her, we need to let them know immediately, and four days is a long delay."

His shoulders fell in defeat. He was failing his friend again, and this time it might cost her her life. He placed his head in his hands and tried to think while Ian activated his security team.

"Thomas."

Her voice was a whisper he almost missed, but it was the fact she'd called him by his first name that caught his attention. When he looked up, he was staring into an intense pair of dark blue-gray eyes. They were full of a furious protective strength that mirrored his own.

"She'll be okay. I don't know Ian's team well, but I know you wouldn't trust them if they weren't good at their job," she said, laying her small hand on his massive shoulder and giving it a squeeze.

The world paused for a moment, and he swore the weight of it lifted from his shoulders for the first time in months.

"Isn't there a bar in this place? I think we could both use a drink."

"There's two actually," Ian said as he strode back into the room. "The main bar by the pool and the cigar lounge. There's also a restaurant."

Jessica frowned.

"Samantha held out on me," she said.

"How so?"

"She dragged me to the spa, but I openly refused. Then she gave me the general highlights of the place and the private play-spaces in a whirlwind tour until we ended up in an oversize closet. Where she tortured me with clothes."

Both men laughed at the description.

"That sounds like Samantha," Kade said and gave her a wry grin.

"Ian, does your team have the situation handled?" she asked, looking over at him.

"Yes, Ma'am. We're behind the curve here, but there's nothing more we can do until we hear from them."

"Right answer," she replied.

Ian laughed.

"Now Kade, you'll show me where this cigar lounge is because it's been a long week and I need a finger or two of scotch," she commanded.

"Yes, Ma'am," he said as he rose from the chair, shooting Ian a preemptive *go to hell* look.

"Now you're catching on."

"Alexandra will love you," Ian said as they passed.

"Won't you join us, Mr. Breckenridge?"

"I'd love to, but I need to be available for updates from the team, and I have other things which require my attention."

"Tell Jillian I said hi," Kade threw at him.

"That's not a good look on you, Kade," Jessica chided.

The words hit him like a ton of bricks. He'd always used cutting sarcasm as a defense mechanism, and never had anyone called him on it. Yet, here was this woman whose approval he craved. Kade wanted to please her in a way he'd never experienced before.

"I deserve it," Ian said, relieving Kade's internal tension a notch.

He tossed Ian a look of gratitude.

"Shall we?" he asked, motioning toward the door.

Jessica nodded.

Not wanting to be in front of her, he laid a hand lightly on her back to offer the directions to their destination. Her warm skin radiated through the material while the thick lacing of the corset reminded him of the glimpse he'd caught earlier. What he wouldn't do to unwrap the package underneath.

CHAPTER TWELVE

Jessica's brain spun as Kade navigated them toward the cigar lounge. Life was much simpler when men came on strong and macho. She could easily categorize them, put up the necessary walls, and plow through whatever issues she faced. It was when they showed emotion or vulnerability that was always her undoing, and Mr. Kinkaid had shown both. There was no doubt he adored the club's owner, but it seemed like an older brother situation, possessive and extremely protective. The thoughts running through her were nothing near the same. His firm hand on her back made her want to know what it would be like to have them wrapped around her. To order him to hold her close and make the world go away.

"Why the cigar lounge?"

At the question she lost her focus and tripped over her own foot. Strong hands grabbed both arms before she splayed against the hard marble floor. Embarrassment at her clumsiness radiated through her, warming her skin. When she recovered her footing, Kade placed his hand on her back once again and navigated them forward without a word.

"Because I learned to smoke cigars early and drink scotch when the 'men' were talking. Over time, it became an indulgence I enjoyed when the world became stressful," she admitted.

"What do you prefer to smoke?"

"I often have simple taste. Something easy like a Drew Estate Isla del Sol or a Macanudo with a Connecticut wrapper."

They continued down the hall a couple of steps in comfortable silence. There was no rush to the questions; rather they were answers to their relevant destination.

"Highland or low-land scotch?"

"Highland. There's something about the smooth caramel creaminess I prefer. Though I've had nothing over a ten-year-old, I've heard some of them are better when aged."

Kade smiled down at her.

"I can confirm it to be true sometimes," he said as they approached the lounge.

He opened the door and stepped aside to let her pass before following her inside.

"Good evening, Mr. Kinkaid. It is good to see you."

Kade smiled at the host as they entered.

"Charles, this is Ms. Lawson. Anything she wants, until further notice, is on the house tab at Alexandra's wish."

"Yes, Sir," he responded and typed the information on the screen in front of him.

Jessica started to object but stopped when Kade shook his head. She noticed a small cord with a thin in-line silver pendant around his neck and made a note to ask Kade its meaning.

"How is Alexandra?"

"She's good and hoping to be back soon."

"Most excellent. We've missed her around here."

Kade nodded at the man.

"Would you prefer open seating or a private lounge?"

"A private lounge, please."

With a couple more taps on the screen, he looked up and smiled at them.

"This way please," he said, stepping in front of them and walking toward the back of the lounge.

Jessica was in awe of the obvious expense poured into the lounge. The dark teal blue walls took the edge off the distinctly masculine room. Everywhere she looked, espresso leather furnishing filled the space. It was cooler than the rest of the club, and she shivered slightly as she adjusted to the temperature.

In one corner a woman knelt between the knees of a man. She was clad only in a small skirt which did little to hide any of her body. Her full breasts jutted forward toward the man as he lay a long cigar ash across them. Along the wall, a group laughed as they each held a long hose from an extravagantly ornate hookah as large billows of water vapor surrounded them with each exhale.

Charles opened a door to an enclosed room about the size of a small bedroom. Two large leather chairs sat on either side of an end table, and Kade motioned to them with a wave of his hand.

"Padron Family Reserve No. 45 Maduro Toro, Mr. Kinkaid?"

"Two please, Charles, and two glasses of Glenmorangie Signet," he said.

"Very good, Sir," he said and gave a slight bow before retreating from the room, closing the door with a soft click behind him.

"Do you always order for others?"

"Did it relieve stress from you and give you a true opportunity to relax in a new atmosphere?"

"Do you always answer a question with a question, Mr. Kinkaid?"

"Are you always so stubborn that the smallest gesture of grace and kindness from a man makes you defensive, Detective Lawson?"

She stood staring at him for a long moment, unable to fully process the words coming out of his mouth. They made her nervous, as if he could see right past her entire collection of mazes and walls and straight into her essence. Everything in her demanded she pull herself together before he thought her a bumbling fool who wasn't in control of her world. Her neck ached from staring up at him, but she refused to be the first one to look away. Power was taken, demanded. Every man in her life had taught her that fact, often the hard way.

Kade was nothing like the men she'd encountered before. He was confident and powerful in his own right, but there was something beneath the surface, a beautiful vulnerability and openness. Neither part diminished the other or the whole.

"Yes," she finally said.

He quirked an eyebrow at her.

"Yes, I am always stubborn and defensive at the slightest kind gesture from a man because I know it is a power move. Something to prove I am less than, weaker or dumber—not that my petite stature doesn't assist them with that assessment."

Kade frowned at her honest response.

"You are an amazing woman and deserve so much more," he whispered and reached up to caress her cheek.

Something in her shifted. Maybe it was the strain of the recent situation or the lack of touch she'd experienced for far too long. She clenched her eyes shut as the unbidden wave of emotion threatened to steal her control. A tear escaped and slid down her cheek. Without a word, Kade's warm thumb wiped it away. Time held no meaning. Somewhere in the darkness, as she attempted to collect her thoughts, a small click of the door opened and closed.

"Kiss me," she commanded.

His lips brushed over her mouth in a slow caress. There was no rush in the movement as his hand snaked behind her neck to support it, relieving the slightest ache. She let her body relax into his while his movements remained unhurried and gentle.

Jessica melted into Kade's touch and forced her tongue between his lips. Logical thought disintegrated in a cloud of lustful images as Kade's other hand cupped her bound waist and pulled her toward him. The bulge of his cock pressed against her thigh, and she moaned into his mouth. Her body trembled under the onslaught of sensation, and his hand tightened on her waist to steady her.

Thick lust rushed through her as she moaned against his mouth.

Her hands slid around his waist unbidden and stroked his skin in time with the parry and thrust of their tongues. Pure need rushed through her like a drowning person on a sinking ship as her mind fought to find purchase in her lusty haze. Kade's head pulled away until the gentle stroke of his tongue seemed like a dream.

"If you continue to kiss me that way and make such beautiful sounds, I am not sure I'll be able to stop myself from pleasuring you until you scream my name," Kade said against her lips, his breath coming in long pants mirroring her own.

The words gave her mind purchase, and she stepped back until they were no longer touching. Need flowed palpably between them, and neither spoke. Between her legs, the thin lacy panties were soaked, and she only hoped the pungent air in the cigar lounge covered the scent of her arousal.

She ran her hands down the front of her pants suit to find center. Then with a slight nod, she lifted her chin to look up into his lust-filled gaze.

"I see our order has arrived. Will you please light my cigar, Mr. Kinkaid," she said in an attempt to show indifference to the previous situation.

"My pleasure to be of service, Detective," he replied, parroting her tone.

JESSICA TOOK A SEAT ON THE FARTHEST CHAIR AND WATCHED AS Kade clipped the end of the cigar. Then he carefully roasted the tip before lighting it. Each move was like an elegantly choreographed dance. Each one had a purpose, but it was the execution of them which held her rapt attention. When he blew on the end of the cigar and it glowed an even ring of red, he presented it back to her. With a satisfied smile, she took a long puff, letting the flavorful smoke roll around her mouth before exhaling it in a small cloud which rose above her head.

"Please join me," she said, lifting her chin toward the other cigar lying on the silver salver atop the table.

With the same care, Kade lit his cigar. This time, instead of blowing on the tip of the cigar to light it, he took several long draws until the tip glowed a bright cherry red.

"It looks like you've had quite a bit of practice lighting cigars," Jessica observed.

"My background has given me training in several areas of life. One of my past Mistresses preferred to never light her own cigar," he said without elaborating and took a deep draw on the end of the stick.

"You identify as a submissive?"

"Yes. Though I am unsure why it surprises you."

"My encounters with the rare submissive male in my world have all been very focused on what I could do for them. It was like they felt I was a fetish dispenser because I was female and dominant. There was always a lack of respect in the situation," she said, unable to hide the disgust and irritation.

"People often forget the underlying factors and only want the fun kinky bits," Kade said in agreement, a ring of smoke falling out of his mouth with each word.

"You seem different," she said, cocking her head slightly as if the change in perspective would give her a better understanding.

"We all approach our preferred points of view in a variety of ways. I'm sorry your past experiences were less than desirable."

"How do you see such a dynamic then, Mr. Kinkaid?"

He shrugged before answering the question.

"It's simple. A dynamic relationship is naked honesty wrapped in vulnerability served in devotion and surrender. The lucky ones are based in love."

"If only the world were so simple," Jessica said wistfully.

"When you drop the drawbridge, then someone can help you slay the dragons because we all need help. It's a lesson driven home for me quite recently. When we lock others out in our greatest moment of need, we not only crush ourselves but those around us."

There was a sadness in his voice. She wanted to take it away, but his words struck a dissonance in her own soul that it would be hypocritical to even attempt it.

"True, but the world expects female Dominants to have a cold, aloof persona. One who humiliates and belittles others. Even in my work, I don't find it productive or desirable to treat others in such a way, but far too often I am forced to become one of the guys or a woman they think they can walk all over."

"And what do you desire?"

"To delve into the darkest fantasies and curl up in the most beautiful light," she said wistfully.

Jessica picked up the glass of scotch, suddenly feeling far too vulnerable for her own liking. She took a long sip. The sweet rich scotch played across her tongue like a spicy piece of candy with an aroma that reminded her of a creamy cup of coffee. With a moan she fully enjoyed every indulgent swirl as it worked its way around her mouth.

"That is fantastic," she said when the rich liquid finally snaked down her throat.

Kade smiled in pride and satisfaction. "I'm glad you liked it. Sometimes giving up control gives you far more power to enjoy the experience."

CHAPTER THIRTEEN

Kade loved watching her relax for the first time since they'd met. There was a hint of softness under that hard as nails exterior. He wondered what she'd gone through to make her so afraid of men. It was like watching someone run close to something they deemed dangerous, touch it to see if they would survive, and retreat. It had shocked him when she'd commanded him to kiss her. Those lips were so soft he wanted to linger there until he lost himself in her essence and then move on to explore the rest of her luscious body. His cock twitched at the thought, still at attention from their interaction. In this moment he was thankful for the days of chastity and self-discipline he'd endured in his life.

They sat in companionable silence for a long time, both lost in their own thoughts.

"How did he know where she went?" she asked suddenly.

"I'm not following," Kade said in confusion, lacking the direction of her current thoughts.

"How did Edmund know where Alexandra was located if they didn't plan to meet?"

Kade thought about the question. Edmund had found her in

Boston, but they'd been able to whisk her away to the island before he got there. It frustrated him that he hadn't yet reached Dominick, but he never thought to ask how Edmund knew where she'd gone. Now that Jessica posed the question, he didn't know how he'd missed it.

"I don't know," he said honestly.

"What do you know about Edmund?"

"He's a tech genius with a troubled past. Dr. Jillian Hart was his therapist for the past few years, but HIPAA and patient/doctor confidentiality would make it impossible for her to reveal anything about his past. Someone has told me they sealed his records, so even if she could tell us anything it would be pointless. He's worth more money than a small country, so his resources are unfathomable. Throughout this whole situation, he's been a step ahead..." He trailed off.

"A step ahead?" Jessica prompted.

"Alexandra went to Boston to visit a former mentor and he found her there. According to what you found out, he's now traced her to St. Kitts."

"How many people knew her movements?"

"Less than five."

"Do you trust everyone on that list?"

"With my life," he said with confidence.

"I hope so, because Alexandra's life may depend on it."

Kade nodded. A knot of anxiety formed in his stomach.

"Stop beating yourself up, Mr. Kinkaid," Jessica said softly.

"You said it yourself, her life may depend on the decisions I've made."

"Then she's in good hands. It's everyone else I want to know about," she said.

He watched her take a sip of the sweet scotch and then a long draw on the cigar. The combination was intoxicating. How was it she could make him focus on the most dire circumstances one minute and want to get lost in her in the next?

"There's nothing more we can do about it tonight," Jessica said with an odd finality, draining the last bit of scotch from her glass.

"However, I confess, I've only ever indulged in my proclivities in a home setting. I'm afraid I'll embarrass myself this weekend."

Kade leisurely let a billow of smoke float out of his mouth. In his chest his heart pounded at the possibilities.

"How can I help?"

"Can you show me the equipment that will be available at the event this weekend? I want to be able to make small talk about anything going on. There's nothing better than preparation and a grasp of the social situation to make observing others easier," she said as she stood.

There was a shift in her posture. Her body was more relaxed as she stepped from the room into the larger lounge.

"Thank you, Charles," she said as she passed the host's station.

"My pleasure, Ms. Lawson," he replied with a slight bow of the head.

"Mr. Kinkaid," he said with a knowing smile as Kade passed.

They stepped out into the hallway, and Jessica took a confident lead toward the private rooms in the lower level of the club. With each step he saw the club in a new way. The crack of the whip or paddle slap weren't just a noise in a crowded club where he kept an eye over its participants, but a world he rarely indulged in these days.

"You've learned your way around the halls quickly," he said as they walked down the back staircase.

"A mental map of a place is helpful when you're looking for a way out and not sure what lurks around the corner. A good thing to know in my line of work and it was one of the few places Samantha lingered on today's tour," she said, forcing a smile to cross her face.

Kade chuckled and turned to see Jessica raise her eyebrows in response.

"Samantha was probably hoping to catch Parker down in the halls of the playrooms. He's our local 'artist' and she's got a crush on him," Kade said with a shake of his head.

"How many partners does she have?"

"Depends on the day," he said with a shrug. "She has a husband

and a Dominant who both attempt to keep her in line, a girlfriend she sees periodically, and play partners who are in her general orbit."

"I don't know if I'm envious or astounded."

"It takes a village with that one. She's brilliant in her work, but there are areas where she needs a lot of support. Tough background. We all find our way through our own issues."

Jessica took in the information with a simple nod as they approached the private rooms.

"Where to, Mr. Kinkaid?"

Kade grabbed his phone and swiped through a couple screens before looking up. "Looks like the Sapphire Room is available."

"Lead the way." She motioned in front of her with a wave of a hand. The move pinched her rib, and she grimaced at the pain.

"How are the cracked ribs?" Kade asked as he entered the security code to the door.

"How'd you..."

"You groaned in your sleep when I carried you to bed. Based on my estimate, you took quite a beating. I estimate two cracked ribs, a twisted ankle since you've walked on it all day, and quite the shiner."

"It could have been worse," she mumbled.

She met his hard, protective gaze and held it with one that mirrored it.

"I hope the victory was worth it," he said as he pushed the door to the private room open.

"No comment on how women should be in a less dangerous job, or how my size makes me weaker or less capable?" she said in a cutting tone.

He led them into a room slightly bigger than a normal living room. There were mirrors lining the far wall while dark sapphire blue damask fabric covered the remaining three. In one corner, a dark mahogany St. Andrew's cross sat at an angle while a spanking bench sat in the opposite one. In the center of the room, a large bondage table hung from four thick support chains. The chrome edges glinted under the light of the room.

"You mistake me for an overprotective Neanderthal. I'll give you protective, but I draw the line at Neanderthal. I know some very strong women, and every one of them would kick my ass if I tried to pull that crap. However, it makes me wonder what you're trying to prove."

"Men aren't out to prove anything when they carry the badge," she spat. "Police work isn't all bad guys and bruises. It's solving puzzles. Understanding humans. Thinking through situations."

He watched as her mental armor settled around her, preparing to battle with him.

"According to what I hear you're damn good at your job," he said, moving further into the room.

"I take pride in making sure I'm competent, skilled, and in control of everything I do, Mr. Kinkaid," she said with a smirk.

Her words sent a wave of anticipation running through him as he watched her walk toward the cross.

"Tell me about the St. Andrew's cross, Mr. Kinkaid." She pointed to the large x-shaped piece of bondage equipment in the corner.

"It's a piece of bondage equipment which spreads out a bottom into a slightly off-balanced and vulnerable position. A person can either face forward or place their back against the cross," he said as he walked up behind.

"Please demonstrate," she said with an edge of command in her voice.

"Which way would you prefer I face?"

"Toward me. I want to see what you look like stretched out on it."

Jessica stepped aside as Kade moved to the cross and spread his legs more than shoulder width apart and his arms wide above his head, wrapping his fingers around the outer pegs. A predatorial mask glazed her face while she watched him position himself as she'd requested.

She stepped forward and traced her hand down the muscles of his bicep, letting it continue down his chest until she lay her palm against his stomach. Each touch sent an electric current straight to his cock. His muscles tensed and released as her hand slowly worked toward his cock.

"What I wouldn't give for a knife to cut these clothes off," she said breathlessly, stepping close enough that her breasts brushed against his waist.

Kade's body went taut as the image bloomed. He wanted to let go of the equipment and touch her. Run his hands through her hair until the severe style let go in messy tendrils, but he held still under her touch until he thought he would explode. There was something in the intense way she studied him, like she was memorizing his body with each touch, that made his cock throb hard against the confines of his pants.

"Do you prefer the cross or the spanking bench, Mr. Kinkaid?"

"Whatever pleases you to see me on," he said, holding back a groan.

CHAPTER FOURTEEN

"I'd rather see you on the hanging bench," she said, crooking her finger at him to follow and walked towards the large hanging table in the middle of the room.

Jessica felt him behind her as she made her way across the room.

It'd been far too long since she'd indulged in anything more than vanilla sex. There was something intimate about playing with someone. Watching their breath hitch as the edge of a knife slid down their skin or a well-placed hand ran across a sensitive area. This room was a perfect blend of sex and fantasy. Each piece of equipment was set so one could move between them or be ensconced in an intimate corner with enough room for others to observe.

"It is often better when you experience the equipment yourself. Then you have a better sense of how the body reacts against it," Kade whispered, his breath drifting across the edge of her ear.

It sent a shiver of need through her body. The big man gave her a place where she felt she could breathe without losing her control or power. Arousal shot through her, and she wondered how far she could push the situation. Maybe if she satisfied her curiosity, then she'd settle into the environment.

"If I told you to kneel, how would you respond?"

"There's only way to find out," he challenged.

She stepped to the end of the long, suspended table as the edge of it grazed her ass. Her fingers wrapped around the thick chunk of wood and she took a deep breath. It was one thing to play Dominant in the bedroom as a game and a completely different one to issue a command expecting someone to follow it.

"Kneel in front of me, Kade," she said in a husky whisper.

His large frame came into view in front of her, and he gazed intently into her eyes before sinking to his knees. Kade forced his knees wide and lay his palms up turned on his thighs without taking his eyes off hers.

She gasped at the sight. It was an instant turn-on. He'd given her exactly what she'd commanded, but there was a hint of mischief playing across his face. His chest rose and fell in slow, controlled breaths. It made her smile to know the situation was affecting him as much as it was her.

"If I told you to strip bare, would you?" she asked openly, watching his reaction to the question.

"There's only one way to find out," he said with a smirk.

The power shift was palpable. Here, in this room, they were not equal. Still, if she gave him an inch, she'd bet he'd take over. Kade didn't seem like the *do me* type of male submissive, only in it for his jollies. Nor was there anything weak about him. He offered his power as an exchange. What Jessica wasn't quite sure was what she had to exchange for such intensity and the submission she saw written on his face.

She slid her shoes off and sighed at the softness of the carpet. It felt amazing under her feet as she rotated her sore ankle to relieve some of the pressure. With a careful push, so as not to jostle her sore ribs, she hopped up on the suspended table and looked down at the kneeling form in front of her. For a long moment she thought about her next move. She wanted his hands on her, but there was a line she'd formed in her mind about what was appropriate behavior.

Being undercover this weekend easily blurred them. Jessica needed everyone to believe she was an experienced Dominant in a public setting. Her body wanted her to relieve the tension from the past couple weeks. When this was over, she didn't have to see Kade ever again. She could enjoy the experience for everything it was worth and walk away.

"Do you want to touch me?"

"If it please you," Kade said automatically.

"It pleases me to know if you want to touch me."

A smile curled around Kade's lips. "Yes, Ma'am."

"Where do you want to touch me?"

"Wherever it please you to be touched." He grinned up at her.

"And if I asked how, I suppose it is however it please me," she said and rolled her eyes.

Kade chuckled but did not shift his position.

"You will need original material, Mr. Kinkaid," she said with a sigh.

"As you wish, Ma'am," he shot back in a challenge.

"Let's put that mouth to better use and show me what you can do with it to please me."

Lust filled his gaze, and she shifted back to stretch out on the table. The movement caused it to swing lightly, and she felt like she was floating.

Kade stood and stepped toward her, laying his hands on the table, caging her hips.

"I said nothing about your hands. I said your mouth. Put your hands behind your back." She looked up at him with a devilish smile. Trying to stay a couple of moves ahead of him was a challenge, and she relished a good challenge.

He placed his hands behind his back and bent at the waist. Taking the button of her pants into his mouth, he worked it until it popped free. Then he took the zipper between his teeth and worked it down the track, his eyes trained on hers with each move.

The material lay open at the apex of her legs in a lazy v formation. His warm breath caressed her bare skin. His eyes grazed the exposed patch, and she swore she saw a shiver run through him.

For a lingering moment he hovered right above her body. His eyes were trained on hers while his slow, measured breath stroked the exposed skin. It would be easy to command him to move. To demand he use his tongue to please her. Everything in her wanted to say the words that would make him move and relieve the ache now pulsing between her legs with each heartbeat. But this was a game of wills, and she wanted to see how he played with the minute push-pull of power within an intimate exchange.

Locked in the moment, she silently begged the Universe for him to move. A second later, he pushed his tongue between the opening of the fabric and began to feast. His tongue dipped and teased her clit, sending ripples of pleasure racing through her body. Kade sucked and licked her, teasing her to the edge before retreating to trace the edges of her folds. Need clawed through her. She pushed her hips to meet his mouth and demand more, only to have him retreat until she settled under him and he started again.

She reached for his hair to push him to the perfect spot, only to have him evade her grasp and retreat until her hands rested above her head once again. When his mouth returned, every muscle in her body tightened in anticipation. There was no rush as his tongue flicked against her skin soft enough to drive her crazy and hard enough for her body to demand release.

Kade's tongue circled her clit. Pushing it forward, he probed the edge of her entrance, then sucked the nub, varying the pressure. His face strained in concentration and focus. She knew she wasn't the only one suffering under the weight of his current ministrations.

Pressure grew and waned with each stroke of his tongue. His eyes closed, and his brow furrowed. It was then she knew he was suffering along with her. Jessica pushed her hips up against his mouth. In return, his lips closed around her clit, and he sucked hard, flicking his tongue across the alivened bundle with each breath.

Between one pull and the next, the orgasm took hold and ripped through her in an explosion of release. Hot streams of pleasure raced along every nerve ending. Her back arched off the table as her pussy spasmed in release. A scream ripped from her throat and echoed off the walls. Her whole body shook with the force of the climax. She glanced down between her legs. Kade's hot breath came in pants across her skin, his eyes hooded and glazed over in his own need.

When she floated back to earth, his piercing eyes were staring expectantly at her. His mouth still hovered right above her pulsing pussy, but he didn't move a muscle.

"Kneel." She forced the word out in a whisper between ladened breaths.

Kade slid back into a kneeling position, but his hand remained firmly behind his back as she sat up on the swinging table. Her gaze fell to his groin, and she smiled. The bulge between his legs was rock hard and she could see the slightest throb against the fabric. Jessica was glad to see he wasn't unaffected.

"That was amazing and very pleasing," she said, her voice hoarse.

"Glad to be of service, Ma'am."

She watched him settle below her. His eyes didn't leave hers, and his body didn't move a muscle as he waited on her next command.

"I bet that bulge in your pants would love to be free. Can you imagine how good it would feel to have my hand work up and down the shaft of your hard, throbbing cock?"

Kade moaned in response and his eyes slammed shut.

Jessica slid off the table and stood in front of him, her crotch inches from his face.

"Or to hear me command you to thrust your hard cock deep into my soaked pussy. My warm pussy wrapping around you as you penetrate me with deep, hard, powerful thrusts until it clenches you in glorious spasms, sending you into your own sweet release."

Below her, she heard him groan, but still he didn't move.

"Are you enjoying our dance?" she asked.

"Yes, Ma'am," he ground out between clenched teeth.

"Good. In that case, I know you won't touch yourself or come until our next encounter or three days, whichever comes first," she said.

She held her breath and waited for his answer. For all of her outward confidence, there were times she knew her intensity could push people too far.

"Yes Ma'am. As you wish," he confirmed.

Jessica's heart pounded in her chest. The heady embrace of power filled her, and she smiled. Maybe this assignment wouldn't be so bad after all.

She took a deep breath. Exhaustion swept over her tired body, and she bit back the unexpected yawn.

"Rise," she commanded.

Kade rolled his body back in a motion a dancer would envy. His eyes never left her own, and in seconds he was once again towering over her.

"Thank you, Mr. Kinkaid. Your advice was correct; I believe I understand this piece of equipment more intimately now," she said, patting it with her hand and offering a wry smile.

He nodded in a way that reminded her of a gentleman's bow but short and quick.

The yawn she'd stifled earlier exploded in full force as her face lit in embarrassment.

"Do I bore you, Detective?" Kade quipped with a smirk.

"Hardly."

"I'm honestly surprised you're still on your feet. Based on your injuries and the day you've had here, it is a testament to your fortitude or sheer stubborn will."

Jessica didn't bother to confirm either but dropped her gaze from his before he could glean any more information. When she was weary, her ability to hold a stoic poker face waned in ways that irritated her.

"It's been a long day," she confirmed.

"May I escort you back to the PR's apartment? It makes better sense for you to be on property while you work on your investigation. Maybe you'll take the normal commute time to rest and heal."

While the words were perfectly amiable, it was his change of tone which caught her.

"Was that a command or a suggestion, Mr. Kinkaid?" she asked, looking back up at his face.

"Take it as you will, Detective," he said simply. "Shall we?"

Kade motioned to the door. When Jessica stepped forward, the warmth of his hand radiated across her shoulder. Beside her, Kade's steps were uneven, and she smiled.

"Do you need to adjust something, Mr. Kinkaid?"

"I'd not deign to be so crude, Detective. You created the situation by your own choices and control. Why would I not proudly display it a world that understands?"

His words made her speechless. She was used to men either trying to put her down or calling her a bitch because she was feminine. While she knew she couldn't please everyone, it would be nice to know the rules of the game. Kade wiped her previous rules away and interacted in a way she wasn't accustomed to handling. He might look tame, but she knew without a doubt he'd bite anyone that stepped on his turf wrong.

They walked back up the stairs in amenable silence, the soft click of their footfalls echoing against the walls.

"Is there a significance to the black strand of cord and pendant around Charles' neck?"

Beside her, Kade's steps hit with an uneven staccato, but she didn't look over at him. She knew the question caught him off-guard either because he didn't realize she'd noticed the detail or wasn't expecting her to be so forward with the question.

"Empyrean gives the cord and insignia to submissives who do not have a partner. It places them under the Club's rule. While they are free agents, the club expects a certain decorum and offers protection or assistance in any area they need."

Jessica thought about his statement and its implications.

"Do you wear this insignia?" she asked, suddenly aware she didn't know all the rules of the club.

"I do," Kade stated but didn't elaborate.

"Do partnerless Dominants have any such insignias?"

"They do," he confirmed as they approached the PR firm's door.

The surrounding air seemed oppressing as she turned to him, suddenly unsure of how to end such an unusual day. They stepped into the PR firm's reception area, and Jessica froze.

"It's been a pleasure, Detective," he said, easily smoothing the situation.

Her shoulders fell in relief.

"Likewise. Will you follow my last command?"

"Of course. Where's the fun in the dance if you walk off the dance floor?"

Jessica nodded.

Kade gazed intensely into her eyes and lifted her hand to his lips, placing a soft kiss across her knuckles.

Her heart raced in her chest, and she worked to control her own breath.

"Sleep well, Detective."

"And to you, Mr. Kinkaid."

He opened the door, and when she stepped onto the lower landing of the apartment's stairs, closed it behind her.

"What. The. Fuck. Was. That," she whispered, sagging against the door.

Wisps of power and control buzzed through her chased by physical exhaustion. She pulled herself off the door and climbed the flight of stairs.

On the kitchen island sat a glass of wine and a note.

Hope this helps you rest, Detective.
~Kade

Jessica stared at the wine in disbelief. How? When?

Picking up the glass, she took a sip. The soft, sweet liquid coated her tongue in the perfection. Making her way back to the bedroom, her mind swirled with questions and emotions while her body demanded rest.

As she walked through the door, the lamp lights on either side of the bed lit to a soft glow. On the bed was a small bundle.

Study Materials.
Enclosed you will find your member insignia and club protocols.
Welcome to Empyrean.
~K

Jessica unwrapped the bundle. On top was a black velvet jewelry box. She lifted the lid and a small gasp escaped. A sapphire blue pendent surrounded by the club's name glittered in the soft light. Beside it lay a silver chain and lapel pin holder. The lid's top was emblazoned with the club logo and the word Dominant. This morning she thought she'd known everything there was to know about accepting that role, but now she wasn't so sure.

CHAPTER FIFTEEN

"**K**atie, where are the P&L reports?" Kade said into the phone, his voice terse with frustration and aggravation.

"They are in the third blue folder under the purple folder in the second pile to the right of your desk, Sir," she said calmly, though her tone was laced with its own brand of exasperation.

Kade stared at the three piles on his desk. Never had he experienced a constant bombardment of paperwork from every department. The chef was demanding to know when his food order would arrive, the bar manager wanted to know if the gin was on order, the spa need some type of exotic oil, and the maintenance staff was out of paper towels. In addition, there was an upcoming corporate meeting where he needed to present the most recent profit and loss for the current quarter.

Katie was a godsend in attempting to keep everything organized with some bizarre color-coded system, though none of it was making sense to him. Coupled with the near constant throb in his groin from a true need to release for over two days since Jessica gave the order for him not to come, and he was ready to scream in frustration.

He ran a hard hand through his hair. If he didn't figure out this shit, it wouldn't matter if they got Alexandra in time because there wouldn't be a club left. He still wanted to strangle her for walking away and more importantly for leaving him to be the Master of this ship. His job was the damn director of security, not the service provider for the whole club.

"You made Katie cry, I hear," Ian said, leaning on the doorframe.

"Mr. Breckenridge, unless you have something useful to provide, get the fuck out," Kade growled.

Ian chuckled.

"I see someone needs to save a drowning man."

Kade glared at Ian, then looked down and continued to paw through the well-organized folder for a report he barely understood.

Without a word, Ian walked to the sideboard and poured a finger of scotch and set it on Kade's desk.

"Drink. Then talk," Ian said, pointing to the glass.

Kade's mouth opened, but Ian shook his head and pointed to the insignia on his label. The man almost never wore the Dominant's pin, but the sight of it, and his current turmoil, gave Kade pause. He picked up the dark liquid and threw it back far faster than necessary.

"She should have left you in charge," he said as the liquid burned a path down his throat.

"I've got my own company to run, and she knew you were more than capable of handling it," Ian pointed out.

"Does it look like I'm 'handling it'?"

"No, it looks like you are being far too much like your boss on the outside but do not realize the one thing she knew well-you must rely on the whole team to do their jobs. Make them lift their own area and not dump on you. You aren't the club slave, you are the director of security and current club owner stand-in. Both things you are more than capable of doing."

Kade sighed and stretched. His shoulders ached, and he felt tension in places he'd never experienced.

"This desk job is for the birds."

Ian laughed. "We've all got our place."

"And mine is supposed to be out walking the floor and figuring out how Edmund is constantly one step ahead of us."

"Let the detective lift that one. It's why she's here. She's an expert in her field and according to her background, more than qualified. Speaking of the detective, I heard you gave her a tour of a private room the other night," Ian said, lifting an eyebrow.

Kade rubbed his neck and avoided Ian's gaze. "Something like that," he finally said.

"How'd it feel to kneel again?"

The words stunned him.

"You forgot to turn off the cameras," Ian said to put him out of his misery.

"Fuck. Who was on watch?" he asked, searching for the watch schedule under the piles of papers. Normally his desk was organized to the point he could give minute details about nearly anything going on in the club, but he wasn't even sure where this morning's coffee mug was located.

"Tanner," Ian supplied. "And the minute you hit your knees, he killed the feed to the room."

It wasn't the fact that the staff saw him play, but since they all worked closely together, most of them turned off the cameras when they stepped into a private room. Playing in a public space was one thing, but things could get enormously passionate in more intimate situations.

"It was intense. She's new in some ways. Most of her experiences seem to have been in the bedroom, but she has all the makings..." Kade let the sentence die before he finished it.

"Well, this is an unusual situation," Ian quipped.

"What? I play. Everyone knows the side of the slash I prefer."

"You mean you wear the appropriate jewelry for the club underneath that tie, but no one sees it and you'll only refer to if someone asks. But you've not hit your knees since Katherine, and before that it was what—three years since Alexandra?"

"So?"

"So? You don't hit your knees just because someone said it. If they touch the floor under a command, it's because you wanted them to."

"What? Now you're my therapist?"

Ian shook his head. "I'm a person who's known you longer than all the names I've mentioned and knows many of your darkest secrets. But talking to Jillian might not be such a bad idea."

Kade shot him a look, and Ian threw his hands up in defense.

"Got it. I'll butt out, but don't you dare ruin whatever might be here just because you are scared the woman is in a dangerous job. We can't predict anything-Alexandra was in one of the safest environments possible."

"And look how that's turned out. My watch and I fucked it up," Kade spat.

"You can't fix what you don't know," Ian said in resignation. His own frustration over the situation was written clearly on his face. "This paperwork, however, I can help you wrangle it and get you back on top."

"Now that's the best thing I've heard all day."

FOUR HOURS LATER, THE STACK OF FOLDERS ON HIS DESK HAD diminished to two: the P&L report and a long explanation from Ian on the best way to present it to the investors and the security file for Alexandra. He was exhausted and glad to see the top of his desk.

"Thank you," he said, leaning back in his office chair.

Ian smiled and saluted him with a well-earned glass of bourbon.

"How does that woman do it? More importantly, why?" Kade asked to the air.

"She's a highly organized workaholic who's set processes and teams in place to help her build whatever she dreams up. As to why? She's chasing a ghost."

"Her dad." Kade leaned forward and looked over at Ian.

"Yes. He was a ruthless son of a bitch," he replied, throwing back the last of the bourbon. "He always wanted her to follow in his real estate footsteps. Thought she was a failure because she owned a boutique PR firm. He didn't know she was an author, Dominatrix, or club owner."

Kade nodded.

"I can't get over the fact she didn't tell me what was going on," he said, opening the file on his desk.

"Would you have believed her?"

"I'm the one that intervened when Edmund proposed," he said gravely. "Something in my gut didn't feel right after that, but I had no evidence it involved him in anything but unwanted attention. I even brought that up to her on several occasions."

"Being threatened is scary. She's not the first client to be stupid in the face of danger," Ian acknowledged.

"But I'm not just anyone. I was her former submissive."

"Note the former. Now you are her director of security and close friend. You're at a distance. Not a far one but a distance nonetheless. I don't think she even trusted herself with the situation."

Kade stared out into the room. A jumble of thoughts crowded his mind.

"Do you think you can take over the mentor program with Cassandra?" Kade finally asked.

"Is it based on the club's protocols and rules?"

"It is. Alexandra took her on right before the world blew up. I thought I could take her on, but it's one too many things for me. It's straightforward: set up a weekly check-in, go over the workbook assignments, and test her various skills," Kade said, picking up a folder labeled with Cassandra's name from his side table and walking it over to Ian.

The other man flipped through the folder.

"How often is she on site?" Ian asked, not lifting his eyes from the papers.

"That's another matter. I pulled the access reports for the last three months, and Cassandra's been here an average of five days a week. Her keycard shows most of her visits are in the library, but command has noted she's been in other areas of the building when her last access was there."

"And this makes you suspicious?" Ian queried.

"It's more than that. She showed up at the PR firm the other morning looking for Samantha or Melodie-or at least that's what she said. When I saw her there, she acted odd."

Ian's head snapped up from the pages he was flipping through. "Define odd."

"Nervous. Cagey. She said she wanted to discuss Samantha's point of view for one of her assignments, but those discussions are off-limits at the firm. The clientele might be from all walks of life and alternative lifestyles, but they aren't the only type they cater to."

Ian looked at him thoughtfully.

"Nervous, like *I'm staring down a six foot four well-built man with long hair and tribal tattoos who runs security* or nervous like *Shit, I've been caught, now what do I do?*"

Kade huffed and folded his arms over his broad chest. "I'm not intimidating."

Ian let out a snort at the obvious contradiction.

"It was more the *Shit, someone caught me*," Kade said, glaring at Ian. "She kept putting her hand behind her back, like she was concealing something, but there didn't seem to be anything in her hand."

At Kade's words, Ian scowled. "Have the detective run a deep background on her. I'll see what I can find out when we have our mentor meeting."

"I'll add her to the command's watch list."

Kade grabbed a pen and wrote out the reminder. "Sounds good."

"Okay. Now that this desk is wrangled, I need to get out and do security rounds."

Ian chuckled as he followed him out the door.

CHAPTER SIXTEEN

"Can I get you anything?" the bartender asked as Jessica walked toward the bar stool at the far corner of the bar. She tucked her long skirt under her knees and hooked her heels against the brace of the stool.

"Sparkling water with a lime, please," she said, laying the club protocol book and a notebook on the bar.

"You are starting with the hard stuff, I see," the bartender said with a smile.

"Starting out easy is for wimps," she quipped, a smile crossing her own lips in return.

He sat the drink down on a napkin in front of her.

"You're actually reading that book?" He grimaced, pointing to the large three-ring binder.

"Yes."

"Why? I can boil it down to the following. Use common sense, don't be stupid, and ask first."

"Is that so?" she asked him, puzzled. While he was right that the basics could easily be boiled down into such simple terms, it was the power dynamics and intricacies that fascinated her. The complexly simple interactions between two people in such relationships.

"How long have you worked here..." Jessica let the pause hang in the air.

"Jack. My name is Jack and about three months."

"What do you think of the club owner, Jack?"

"I don't rightly know, as I haven't met her yet. I hear she's out of town, but the management around here is pretty hush about the whole situation," he said as he wiped down the bar.

Jessica took the information and scribbled it her notebook.

"I've heard from some of the members she's tough as nails," she pushed, hoping for some perspective from the staff. Most of them had been very closed off to her questions the minute she probed any deeper than *Hey, this is a great place.*

"That's what the bar manager says. This place has more cleaning lists and checklists than any other place I've worked. But I can't complain none. The pay's better, the scenery can't be beat—or is it that the scenery's taking a beating?" He smirked and nodded to the couple over in the corner.

A woman was bent over an older man's lap, her ass on display and bright red with several handprints. Jessica could hear her soft sobs emanating from the corner, but the woman didn't seem in any distress she didn't enjoy.

"He loves punishing her in public. They come in every few days. Always sitting at the same table. He orders a glass of ice cubes along with a gin and tonic. Then he'll bend her over his lap, flip up her skirt and spank her. When he's done, he'll sooth all those red areas with ice cubes until she's wiggling and squealing under his touch."

Jessica listened to Jack while she took in the scene in the corner. At two in the afternoon, she was sure the place would be dead, but in several corners throughout the club, she'd spied people in intimate moments. Some were like watching her fantasies play out in front of her while others confused her. Regardless, all of them aroused her.

Every turn reminded her of her time in the Sapphire Room. The sight of Kade kneeling in front of her, yet there was a fire in his eyes. She adored the sight. The thoughts send a hot spark of arousal and need through her. Jessica shifted on the barstool and returned her focus to the papers in front of her.

"You know, if you're interested in learning the ropes around here, I'd be glad to show you around when I get off shift," Jack said, giving her a wink and a grin.

"That won't be necessary, Jack," Kade said as he walked up to the end of the bar.

Her heart nearly stopped at the sound of his voice. For two days, she'd busied herself with work and learning everything she could about the club. Every scene reminded her of watching him fall to his knees at her command. She craved to touch him and take him to the edge, waiting on her order.

The two men had an unspoken conversation, and she knew she was the subject. Kade's protectiveness was obvious, but the hint of possessiveness had her curious.

"Maybe next time then." He shot Jessica a smile and nodded to Kade before walking to the other end of the bar.

She flashed Kade a knowing smile as her gaze dropped to his crotch.

"How's life, Mr. Kinkaid?" she said, reaching for her water to quench her suddenly parched throat.

"Strained. And yours, Detective?" he whispered on the edge of a growl.

Jessica turned to face him, her hands inches from his crotch.

She lifted her head. His direct gaze unsettled her, challenging her in a dare to make the next move. Without dropping her gaze, her fingers stroked against the fabric of his slacks. His cock came to life under her touch. She well knew the effect she was having on him, but it was the effect he was having on her that caught her by surprise.

"What if I told you to kneel right here? Would you drop to your knees?"

Her fingers continued to tease along the edge of the fabric, but her gaze never left his.

"Fortune often favors the bold, Detective," he said with a slight smirk.

"Does it now, Mr. Kinkaid?" she asked, letting her fingers cup under his balls and squeeze.

"Indeed."

His voice was strained. She watched him fight the shiver of pleasure and struggle for internal control.

"There's always a possibility I would follow the command," he said with a hissed exhale. "Which also means there's a possibility I wouldn't."

"So how do I know which one you'll choose?" she asked, her fingers releasing his balls and working their way back up his cock as it strained against the fabric.

"You take a chance, Detective."

He braced a hand on the bar and leaned in toward her, bringing his lips within a whisper of hers, hovering just out of reach. Their breaths mingled in an intimate confession neither voiced.

"Put your hands behind your back, Mr. Kinkaid." She forced the whispered words between her lips.

Kade responded. His hand lifted from the bar and linked with the other behind his back, but the distance between them did not change.

"I confess your advantage in these situations. I am behind in knowing all the intimate rules to these public games."

"Then be brave enough to dance, Detective."

Jessica's breath hitched at the words. Between them her hand paused and drew a moan from Kade.

"I need to learn the ins and outs of the dynamic interactions. How do I learn everything to get on top? Who will teach me what I need to know?"

She watched Kade's eyes fall closed, but the rest of his body was a rigid, unmovable object. A storm of emotions played across his face.

When his eyes snapped open, he watched her with an intensity she'd never experienced.

"Me."

The word was an answer. A statement. A challenge.

"And what do I get out of it, Mr. Kinkaid?"

White hot fear mixed with her arousal, pushing her to the edge of her own control. The air was heavy. Every inch of her lit up with a burning need to possess him.

"The potential for trust, loyalty, and a deep, unique intimate bond. The Dominant isn't the only one who can guide and teach in a relationship. It's like a dance teacher who teaches the lead the steps. Just because they look like they are following doesn't make it less. When the lead finally has the steps down, the dance changes again."

A delicious shudder shot through her at the thought. Kade was all hot, hard, exquisite specimen of a man, and here he was throwing down the gauntlet, daring her to command him for their mutual pleasure.

"It's a power exchange-and I bring my own power. Do you?"

The challenge of his words pushed past her hesitation. Having her power challenged was one of her greatest weaknesses. Throughout her life everyone had underestimated her.

She straightened her shoulders, and a smile curled across his lips.

"Mr. Kinkaid, please gather my things. Let's dance," she commanded, hoping he would follow. Her heated gaze matched his, and neither moved for a long moment.

Finally, Kade stepped back and gave her room. Jessica breathed a controlled sigh of relief and slid off the bar stool, making her aware of their significant difference in height and thankful she'd worn heels. Her skirt fanned out as she spun on her toes. Without looking back, she stepped past him and continued down toward the bar's entrance. Behind her there was a quick shuffle of papers. Before she reached the door, Kade's footfalls matched her own.

JESSICA PUSHED ON THE DOOR TO THE SAPPHIRE ROOM. ITS familiarity gave her confidence, but the nerves in her stomach ran rampant. Behind her, she heard Kade set down her notes and then step close enough that she felt his breath on her neck.

"Let me introduce you to the studio before we begin our dance," he said.

Kade led her to the control panel, explaining each of the buttons for lighting, audio, and security. Pushing open the cabinet doors along the wall closest to the door, he showed her the available toys and then grabbed his keys and unlocked a lower drawer.

"A supply of my own things is in here," he said, pointing out an array of ropes, gags, and a crop.

"Quite forward, Mr. Kinkaid."

He shook his head in denial. "They are always in here. It is my private locker."

Realization dawned through her. He'd chosen this room on purpose.

"Why this room?" she asked with trepidation.

"It is one of two rooms I've never played in as a submissive. It is the only room in the club where I'd never played until the other night."

His words were full of unspoken meaning, and she worked to piece it all together.

"According to your skills assessment, you know the basics of rope groundwork, good knife control, wax play, takedown play, and obviously chastity. You lack skills in most impact skills, but passed all safety assessments on bondage."

Jessica blinked at his technical assessment. The change from the challenge in his eyes at the bar made her second-guess their interaction.

"Based on your skill, I am comfortable with rope, a basic level of chastity, as you've already shown a preference, and any other form of bondage you would prefer. Your strong personality is more than up to the task of mental control," he said with a smirk. "Safe sex supplies are in the middle drawer of the counters."

Her thoughts raced. What was she thinking? She might issue the commands, but he was in control. Could she learn this intricately balanced dance or were the men in her world right? Jessica grit her teeth against the invasion of a lifetime of being told she was less than or not up to the task.

"It's a lot to take in," she said, the nerves obvious in her own voice.

"I believe in you," Kade breathed, his voice barely above a whisper.

She watched him step back and assume an at-rest posture, his hands behind his back, feet shoulder width apart, hands clasped at his lower back, but his eyes remained trained on her. Everything in her world had led her to this moment when she either stepped up to what was offered or shut up and realized many of the things she'd heard throughout her life were true. It was one thing to initiate in bed. It was quite another to take control and power in a relationship and wield it for the benefit of both.

The big questions could wait for now. Watching Kade waiting on her next word was intoxicating. Pure need and desire danced in his eyes, echoing her own, even if his stance was in the form of patiently waiting for her next move.

CHAPTER SEVENTEEN

His heart hammered in his chest. Her fear was almost palpable, but it was the determined look on her face that gave him hope. It took a certain confidence to play with a dynamically charged relationship. Many thought they could handle it, but so often it fell apart when the balance of power shifted in an uneven fashion, and still other relationships never developed outside of play. Their physical attraction was obvious. Her next steps determined how they proceeded.

Jessica reached into his drawer and pulled out several skeins of rope. Then she opened the center drawer and grabbed condoms. His cock jumped at the possibilities.

"There's a lounge in the far corner. Please bring it to the center of the room, Mr. Kinkaid."

She'd issued the order without looking up. He saw her bite her lip in trepidation, but it was her fortitude to move forward which drew his admiration.

Kade walked over and pushed the curved chair into the center of room. Its design allowed for it to support a person in many positions. Underneath the frame there were several places to tie someone down or attach a clip with cuffs. The height of the chair back swept easily down the face into a low curve which cradled the body. Once the chair was situated, he fell back into a parade rest stance and waited.

"Rope. Its application is an art form," she said, running the rope through her hands as she unwound it from the sailor's coil. "There's something about it. Knowing it winds its way around the most private parts of a person. Or using it to bind limbs to immobilize. Once in place it is beautiful and deadly. Like most things in life, people often underestimate it based on size and familiarity."

Her words punctuated each step. Images bloomed across Kade's mind. Anticipation pulsed through him with each heartbeat.

"For nearly three days, you've waited," she said, approaching him and laying the rope and condoms on the chair. "You filled those days with work and people but, if I were to ask, did your thoughts stray far from me?"

His cock jumped at her words. She was right: the last three days without release had been filled with near constant thoughts of the detective and their last encounter. He kept hoping to run into her or find her walking into his office with a piece of information or even a command. The near constant arousal set him on edge with need, even with a large concentration of self-discipline.

"No, Ma'am."

"While I may be new to this version of a dynamic, such a thing would be desirable for someone in my position-isn't that correct?"

"If it pleases you."

Her fingers worked the buttons. There was no rush in her movement as she worked her way down the front of his shirt. His nipples hardened at her nearness. Jessica pushed the shirt off his chest, letting her fingers graze the edge of his taut nipples.

He moaned in response. She gave him a playful smirk and licked her lips before reaching for the button at the top of his fly. Kade involuntarily inhaled in anticipation. Under her insistent fingers, the button popped free, and she tugged at the zipper. Once it reached the bottom of its short path, she pressed the fabric back, and his hardness sprang free from the confines of his pants.

"I love a man who goes commando-it makes for much easier access."

A shudder shot through him as her hands pushed down his pants, confining his legs in the tangle of fabric.

"I bet you are praying I will wrap my hand around your erection, ending the long hours you've gone without touch. Or maybe I'll see how you taste, returning the favor from my first tour in this very room."

Kade's tormented groan begged her. His eyes were clamped shut, head back and mouth open, but he remained still.

She grabbed a condom from the chair, tore the wrapper with her teeth, and waited. A tremble of need ran through his legs.

"Look at me," she ordered.

His head dropped immediately, and he opened his eyes. A raging beast of need clawed its way through him, but he refused to give in to it. With an intent look, he watched her slowly roll the condom down his length.

Lust burned through him. *Touch me,* he wanted to scream but remained silent. She wrapped a slender hand around the head of his erection and gave a gentle squeeze. His cock came alive in her hand. Making a fist around his shaft, she moved down and released him. He bucked forward, silently begging for her touch.

Jessica took a quick step back, leaving him hungry in his wanton desire.

"Don't go anywhere," she said and turned to walk back to the front of the room.

His gaze followed her swaying hips. Her firm, pert ass called to his lust-filled mind.

"Stop looking at my ass and strip, Mr. Kinkaid," she said without turning around.

The words took time to register in his lust-saturated mind. His hands moved by their own volition, frantically tearing at the fabric and as he toed off his dress shoes. His cock throbbed, and he forced his focus elsewhere to resist the urge to touch himself.

"Somebody's eager... or desperate," she said, looking down at the pile of clothes.

"Yes, Ma'am."

"I don't know who trained you, but I would be shocked if that pile of clothes was acceptable," she scolded.

Embarrassed, he knelt to pick up the clothes. With painstaking care, he folded each item like he'd been taught years prior and placed them in a small bundle.

"Stay there. Place your arms by your side."

He obeyed without hesitation. Her soft hands glided against his skin as she wound the blood red rope in an intricate pattern around his skin. The harness tightened and braced his arms against his body. Each tie of the knot pushed him deeper down. It was far too long since he'd allowed himself to experience this kind of drop.

He imagined a harness under his clothes or the hardness of a chastity cage locking his cock until she set it free with a key dangling between her full breasts. The thoughts threatened to take him to possibilities which couldn't exist. She was learning what it felt to be a Dominant in this community. He was nothing more than her test subject. Getting too close was dangerous, and falling for her wasn't in the cards.

She pulled on the ropes. They bit into his skin. The sensation drove him further into subspace. His cock pulsed in time with his heartbeat. He was very much a fly caught in a very nice web.

"How does it feel?" she asked, pulling hard on the last knot.

"Good."

Jessica reached for the packet of lube on the chair and ripped open the top. She squeezed the entire contents into her hand and closed her fist to distribute it. Looking directly into his eyes, she fisted his cock, squeezing the base and milking it until a drop of moisture glistened at the top of the condom.

"Nice."

Kade moaned and then she saw a smirk cross his face.

"Care to share your thought with the rest of us?" she said, tightening her hand around his cock and circling the tip with her thumb.

"I..." he gasped. "I was just wondering if it was a good size."

She stopped her motion and looked up at him in confusion.

He sighed at the slight reprieve.

"You said when we met that my original equipment couldn't be altered to suit, so you hoped it was a good size. I was just wondering if it pleased you, Ma'am."

A smile curled on her lips.

"I guess we'll find out if I sink it deep into my hot, wet pussy or maybe I'll leave you to suffer. We'll only know if it pleases me if I choose to fuck you."

He wanted to beg, but he remained stoic and silent.

"Please have a seat, Mr. Kinkaid. We're just getting started," Jessica said, pointing to the large curved chair and bracing against his arm as he rose to help him balance.

Jessica watched him settle onto the large curved chair. His bound arms were a work of art. The weave of the rope across his skin was beautiful. She'd never appreciated the intensity of leading a scene. Even with unsure steps, he was the consummate teacher. If she misstepped or paused, he waited. It was intoxicating and arousing. Watching his reaction to her command or touch sent her mind in a spiral of dangerous thoughts like seeing her name on the pendant hanging from the cord on his neck. Or the feel of a key to his chastity cage resting between her breast under a vanilla suit.

Each image threw fuel on her raging arousal. With her dry hand, she slipped her delicate lace panties down her legs. Then she pulled up the edge of her skirt and let her lube-slicked hand slide between her thighs. She played with her slick folds and let her fingers encircle her clit before giving it a hard pinch. The bundle of nerves screamed in pain until they released in a glorious pleasure. Kade made a pained noise in response.

"Someone likes a little pain," Kade observed, intently watching her hand move. "It will be a pleasure to give you what you need."

Fire shone in his eyes as he gazed at her.

"Imagine your cock being permitted to slide right here, Mr. Kinkaid," she said, dipping two fingers into her pussy. With deliberate strokes, she pumped in and out, never taking her eyes off of Kade's face.

"Please," he rasped.

His hips jerked forward. The veins in his forearms popped under the pressure as he pushed against the ropes. Kade's breath picked up the pace as she stroked herself. She was so aroused she could barely think. Everything in her wanted to sink his cock deep into her, but the game was too much fun to end.

"I want to kiss you," she said, leaning forward.

She crawled her way up his body and braced herself against the large lounge chair, her hands on either side of his head. Jessica brushed her mouth over his. His soft lips were heaven, and she licked across them. She ground against him, his cock lying against the crack of her ass. His lips were warm and welcoming as he opened to her exploration. Her tongue slipped into his mouth, devouring him. She growled as pleasure pulsed through her veins.

Jessica wound her fingers in his long hair and tugged. Kade stilled under her touch, and she made note of his reaction, taking advantage and plundering his mouth with hers until the tension between her legs demanded to have him inside her.

When she released him, she saw the clouded haze of sexual need in his eyes. She eased her body down his. Jessica straddled him and ground her hips against his length. Kade's eyes closed, and his jaw tensed in a combination of pleasure and self-control.

"Don't you come. If I explode in pleasure and milk your cock for all it is worth, you will not come."

"Yes, Ma'am," he ground out.

She hovered right above his eager cock until his eyes opened and his heated gaze was on her. Then she eased herself down his hard shaft. Each inch pushed against her tight pussy as his cock stretched her, filling her completely. Pleasure rippled through her as she held him inside.

"No matter what happens, do not come," she commanded.

"Yes, Ma'am," Kade said, the words forced through his gritted teeth.

Jessica flipped her skirt to cover where they joined. She leaned forward and braced her hands on his muscular chest, caressing his nipples. His hard length pulsed against her pussy in rhythm with his heartbeat. Under her touch he shuddered with pure need and lust. She squeezed the muscles in her pussy around his cock, and he moaned.

"You're killing me, Detective."

"That sounds like a you problem, Mr. Kinkaid," she said.

A smile played on the edge of her lips as she lifted her body until the head of his cock grazed her entrance.

"Is this better?"

"No! Please!"

"You aren't enjoying our time?"

"Yes. I need to come, please," he pleaded.

She let her hips drop enough to tease the head of his cock and then lifted back up. The muscles in her legs screamed with effort, and her own arousal demanded she take him hard, but there was something exquisite in their mutual torture. Her hips continued to dip and lift, taking him in a little deeper, only to return to more shallow movements.

"Fuck! Jessica, please," he said.

The pained look on his face proved he was fighting his own release.

"My, my. Someone's decorum goes out the window when he's in need."

He stared at her incredulously but did not move. His jaw strained against the sensations. She knew his cock ached for release, but the power and control of the situation stoked her own desire. A wave of command and sexual aggression moved through her body. In one smooth motion, she plunged down his cock until he was seated inside of her again.

"Brace yourself. Remember my standing order," she reminded him before lifting her hips until he was almost all the way, and then slammed her hips down, driving him deep into her.

A scream of pleasure ripped from her throat. She slid back up and took him again. Underneath her, Kade snarled and pressed against the ropes. His breath came in pants as she rode him in a merciless rhythm, taking exactly what she needed and in a way she wanted. He was hers to command.

Jessica ground hard against him, forcing her body to clench around him, even when the depth of the movement stung. Pain and pleasure mixed until it was a wave she could not control. The heat of sexual need built between her legs until she could no longer hold it at bay. Her body tensed, and the orgasm sent flames of pleasure racing through her. Jessica bucked and writhed on his cock in disjointed movements as overlapping waves of pleasure crashed against her senses.

"Come for me, Kade," she cried out as her orgasm surged and ebbed.

A guttural sound ripped from his throat, and he thrust his hips up to meet her. She met his driving rhythm beat for beat. Below her, Kade's breath came in pants to match her own. A second orgasm overloaded her system, washing the reason from her mind, leaving raw need in its wake. Jessica thrashed and moaned in the abandonment of her own climax when she heard Kade's growl of pleasure echo off the walls. His body jerked hard, every muscle tight as he stiffened and convulsed, pouring himself into her. She felt his hot cum wash against the condom as her body milked every drop from him.

She sucked in air. Her bones felt like liquid as she fell forward against his chest with a heavy sigh of contentment. Kade's heartbeat thudded against her hand, the spice of his cologne mingled with his own musky scent filling her nose. Right here was perfect. The only thing better would be to feel his arms around her.

Jessica forced the languid desires aside and moved off of him. Walking over to the cabinet by the door, she grabbed a towel and two bottles of water.

"Thank you," he croaked as she approached.

Kade worked his body against the design of the chair until he was upright. Jessica reached between his legs and cleaned up their mutual pleasure with the towel, removing the condom. Then she turned her attention to the rope, working the knots and ties until she released his arms. She massaged across his shoulders and arms to help return the circulation to the abused limbs. Then she wrapped her hands around his waist and kissed between his shoulders.

"Let me take care of you, Ma'am," his said, his voice rumbling through his chest.

Jessica nodded against his back, too exhausted to speak, leaning back against the bench to free his movements.

Kade stood and stretched, then leaned down and scooped her up into his arms, cradling her against his chest. He walked across the room, knelt, and deposited her on a blanket in the corner surrounded with pillows of every shape and size. He propped her against a pillow and smoothed her skirt around her leg. When she was settled, she watched him walk back to retrieve the water.

His naked form was magnificent. Dark tribal tattoos ran across his back, meeting the edge of his long hair, now tussled and no longer perfectly contained in its leather tie. The juxtaposition to her own clothed body brought a smile to her face. She'd never had sex clothed before, and there was something intriguing about it.

Kade returned and waited just off the blanket.

"Hold me, please," she whispered.

With practiced form, he fell to his knees and crawled the short distance to her. Once settled, she climbed into his arms, and he engulfed her. A peace she'd never experienced descended over her.

"Thank you, Kade," she said as her fingers traced the rope patterns imbedded in his skin.

CHAPTER EIGHTEEN

Jessica poured a cup of French press coffee into her cup, savoring the aroma as the steam wafted toward her. Her body hurt. The pain in her ribs from her time with Kade was back with a vengeance; she must remember ecstasy was no excuse to punish her body.

She prayed the caffeine would help her brain fog from far too many things happening at once and give her a bit of focus and concentration for the task at hand. In front of her, piles of paper with smaller sticky notes littered the large island in her temporary apartment. This situation was driving her a little crazy. While Ian and Kade had shared some information, there were so many questions. She didn't know if they were deliberately omitting things or if they thought she didn't need to know. None of it made sense. Why would someone stalk the club owner? More importantly, why did she think running away was the best answer? In between each thought, her scene with Kade flashed through her mind, making concentration next to impossible.

A hard knock on the apartment door pulled her out of her reverie. Jessica picked up the tablet in front of her and swiped the home automation application. Samantha's smiling face appeared on the screen and she swiped to activate the lock. Seconds later, she came bounding up the stairs.

"You have coffee! Thank God. The boys kept me up to all hours of the night, not that I'm complaining, cause I'm not, but I'm beat. If Atlas doesn't get her ass home soon, I'm going to kill her. This workload is impossible," Samantha said as she grabbed a mug and poured a cup of coffee.

"Where is your illustrious business partner?" Jessica asked over her own mug, trying to keep her tone light and uninterested like she was making conversation.

"Out on business," Samantha said, shuttering the edge of her emotion, but her poker face was lacking.

The worry lines on her face were clear.

"Ah. I'm sure she'll be back soon."

Samantha nodded absently, her brows furrowing in thought. Seconds later, a new emotion masked her face, and she smiled over at Jessica.

"Rumor has it a certain detective and a certain director of security are having a fling," she said excitedly.

"Rumors are things bored people start to help fill their empty lives," Jessica replied and let her eyes fall to the papers in front of her.

"According to Tanner, he knelt for you."

"He's a submissive. I am sure when he plays, he hits his knees as part of the game. Mr. Kinkaid has been instrumental in helping me understand the nuances of this most enigmatic world," she replied impassively.

"Bullshit."

Jessica's eyes shot up and stared at Samantha. "Excuse me?"

"You heard me. We don't know each other well, and I know you are new to a more uninhibited world, but let me make something clear-there are those for whom the dynamics of a relationship is a very serious thing. They do not perform like trained monkeys for the entertainment of others. If they do something, it is because it was an active choice. Kade hasn't hit his knees for anyone in over three years. He's only had two Dominants in his life, and the last one nearly destroyed that part of him."

Her words cut through Jessica like a hot knife. Their time together had been eye-opening to her, but she thought Kade was simply indulging her. Indulging in mutual enjoyment while teaching her to dance, as he put it.

"I see," she replied but offered none of the inner questions in her tone.

"Sorry. I'm not usually like this. I've always been the happy free spirit, but all this work is making me part of the commercial complex —and it's making me cranky. Even my Dominant talked to my husband about it," she said, rubbing her ass involuntarily at the obvious memory.

"Does Tanner tell everyone about everything his boss does?"

Samantha laughed. "No. Kade, Atlas, and I have been friends for so long, everyone always assumes we simply know what the others are thinking. Kade's like the big brother I never had. You know the kind-picks on me mercilessly and protective as hell. He's like having a pet tiger. You think he's all calm and controlled until someone walks into his yard, then he eats them."

"Are we talking about the same Kade? I'll grant you the size is intimidating, but he's been nothing less than a gentleman or a man frustrated in the ability to help his friend."

Samantha stared at her as realization dawned. "Well, well—he's got it bad. Please don't break him, Detective."

Jessica shook her head at the implication.

"I can't break something I don't own, Ms. Kingston."

"Beware the white rabbit, Detective Lawson. Not everything on this side of the looking glass is what it seems, but I can tell you the consequences are very real if you get it wrong."

Jessica forced a smile to relieve the edge of tension in the room. "Thank you for the advice. I was wondering if you could help me with something."

Samantha lifted a brow as a question.

"My body is full of knots, my nails are a mess, and this hair will not do if I'm going to be presentable at this big event tomorrow. Do you think you can help me out?"

Excitement bloomed across Samantha's face. "Leave it to me," she exclaimed. "We'll hit the spa for a full treatment. It's one of my favorite things to do before a big event. I'll even grab a nice bottle of bubbly from Alexandra's stash-to help relieve some stress, of course."

She grinned over her mug as she took a long pull.

SAMANTHA LED THE WAY BACK INTO THE HALL AND TOWARD THE club, her mood slightly somber.

"What happened when your husband and your Dominant talk?" Jessica asked.

Mid-step, Samantha paused and worked to maintain her composure.

"It's never good when those two gang up on me. My husband is frustrated because I'm stressed out, working all the time and not focused on all the normal things I do around the house. My Dominant said I was snarky, and for some unknown reason, they both agreed I have an attitude problem," she said, adding an eye roll for emphasis.

"Are they jealous of one another?"

"Sometimes. When time gets imbalanced, someone falls out of another relationship or any other human reason, but most of the time it's a nice situation."

Jessica tried to imagine a relationship with multiple partners and shook her head. She had enough trouble trying to keep her job and her relationships from running over one another. There was no way she could handle more than one at a time.

"I'm in awe at how you juggle it all," she said.

Samantha looked over and smiled at her as they rounded the corner.

"Well, here we are-let's hope Kade didn't take away my access," she said conspiratorially.

Placing her finger on the pad under the placket marked *Wine Cellar*, she was rewarded with a green light and an audible click.

"Yes!"

Jessica smiled at her obvious enthusiasm and followed her inside. The sight that greeted her was nothing short of overwhelmingly extraordinary. Shelves lined the space from floor to ceiling. Each one housed so many bottles she didn't want to imagine the carnage if one of them tipped over. As they walked deeper into the cellar, two small barrels and high stools came into view.

"Welcome to the Empyrean Wine Cellar, or as I refer to it, Alexandra's personal stash. She keeps some of the most expensive wines on the market down here. I try to help with wine rotation as often as possible," she said with a grin.

"Wine rotation?"

Samantha nodded and pulled a bottle off the shelf.

"You know-quality control. I pick a bottle, drink it, and now there's a rotation of a new bottle to fill its place."

Jessica laughed. "And what does Alexandra think of your personally appointed position?"

"She's not amused. But she's not here. So-I think it entitles us to pick from the stock of bubbly in the sparkling wine section, although there is an actual French champagne over there should you prefer it," she said, walking toward the back of the cellar.

"Why does she have so many wines?" Jessica called after her.

"Because this club hosts some of the most powerful and richest clients in the DC area, who happen to also have a propensity for other things, Detective Lawson," a deep male voice said from behind her.

Jessica whipped around and ran straight into a solid wall of muscle. The mix of his spicy cologne and masculine scent filled her nose. She could get used to him towering near her or scooping her up and holding her close. Most of the time men of such a height difference annoyed her and sent her defenses on high alert. Kade, however, did the exact opposite.

"I presume Samantha is down here somewhere," he said with a cocked eyebrow.

"She's somewhere that way." Jessica hitched a thumb over her shoulder.

Kade gazed down at her with a heated look somewhere between annoyed and aroused.

"Jessica, I think this will be the perfect..." The words died on Samantha's lips as she approached.

"The perfect what, Ms. Kingston?" Kade asked over Jessica's head.

"The perfect way to help the detective relax. I heard she had quite the night and with her ribs hurting this morning, I thought..."

"Detective Lawson-why do your ribs hurt this morning?" Kade demanded.

Jessica looked up at him, this time returning her own brand of annoyance.

"Mr. Kinkaid, I appreciate the concern, but my ribs are my issue."

Kade took a deep breath and let it out in a controlled huff. "Ms. Kingston, the cellar isn't your personal wine store. You've visited down here fifteen times in the last month. I appreciate the extra work you are putting in, but I will not be the one answering to Alexandra when she sees the overruns and price," he said, leveling a glare at her.

"Kade," she cooed. "She owes me, and this is a small price to pay for all my worry and concern, not to mention the extra workload for A—" She stuttered to a stop when Kade shook his head in a quick snap to signal no.

Jessica furrowed her brow. They were leaving her out of something. How the hell did they expect her to do her job if they left out details?

"I know, Samantha, but you can very well handle the situation,"

Kade said with assurance. "But this is your last bottle. I'm changing the access today."

"Kade," Samantha whined behind Jessica.

"How did you know we were down here, Mr. Kinkaid?"

He had the good sense to look sheepish. "The security system alerted me."

"And where were you when the alert happened?"

A long pause pervaded the space.

"Yeah, Kade, how'd you get here so quick?"

"I was doing rounds," he shot back at Jessica.

"Is that what they call following us?" Samantha said with a slight pout.

"Samantha," Kade barked, "continue with this incessant irritation and I'll make a phone call I'm sure you won't appreciate."

"You wouldn't dare," she mumbled.

"Try me."

"Children," Jessica interrupted.

Kade glared down at her, and she was positive Samantha was doing the same.

"I want to go to the spa and be tortured with my hair and nails. Could you two please settle this later?" she demanded.

"Yes, Ma'am," Samantha responded from behind her, and Jessica smiled at the show of deference.

In front of her, Kade stood stoically and crossed his arms.

"Detective, why didn't you inform me you were hurting?"

"Mr. Kinkaid..." she started.

"Don't, Detective. Don't you dare dismiss me. It's called an exchange, and it goes both ways. I'll ensure the spa knows the situation and will have relief medication delivered upon your arrival."

He held her with his eyes, and she returned a challenging stare.

"I'm not your responsibility," she breathed, slightly intimidated by his forceful concern.

"You're in my house, you're my responsibility."

"Is that the only reason?" Jessica asked, her curiosity piqued from her earlier conversation with Samantha.

"Not even close, Detective, but we'll leave it for another time."

With that, he pivoted and walked out the door without another word.

"Tiger. You might want to find a leash unless you plan to train him to be good at liberty," Samantha quipped as she walked around Jessica's unmoving form, a wine bottle grasped in her hand.

"They are all going mad," she mumbled to herself as she exited the cellar.

"No, they lack good leadership... Detective, isn't it?"

Jessica startled at the unfamiliar woman's voice and shut the door behind her as she turned and faced her in the empty hall.

The woman's face fell in disappointment as she stared at the closed door.

"Yes. And you are?"

"You can call me Cassandra," she said, shoving her hand forward in a gesture for a handshake.

"Chaos can ensue for a time when a strong, capable leader needs to attend to other things, but I don't think they lack leadership, as you imply. It seems to me Mr. Kinkaid is an accomplished leader."

Cassandra laughed. The noise made Jessica uncomfortable because it sounded somewhere between maniacal and annoyed. Jessica raised an eyebrow in response.

"Kade? He's a freaking submissive. Ultimately he wants to be told to snap to and fall to his knees to anyone who commands it. He's not fit to lead because he'd rather be led."

Jessica shook her head. "How long have you known Mr. Kinkaid?"

"Long enough to know he's not up to the challenge of running this club," she said haughtily.

There was something about the woman that sent Jessica's senses on high alert. Nothing about her, other than her height, should cause the visceral reaction, but she'd learned long ago to pay attention when something felt off.

"Then I doubt you know him well," Jessica shot back, annoyed anyone would question Kade's ability to do his job. "Mr. Kinkaid is up to the challenges in front of him. I am positive Alexandra would not leave someone in charge of her club she didn't feel could perform under pressures."

The other woman leaned a shoulder on the wall and crossed her ankles. "Interesting."

Jessica jutted her chin forward and pulled to her full height.

"What, pray tell, do you find so interesting?" she shot back.

"The fact you have a need to defend him. Jack said you two looked intense at the bar the other day, but he's new-everything seems intense to him. So I wanted to see for myself," she said, shrugging her shoulders.

Jessica clenched her jaw. It was a wonder anything was kept a secret around here, except all the information she needed to know.

"Mr. Kinkaid is assisting me in understanding this community for my work."

Cassandra laughed.

"Is that what they call dominating a man now? Was he assisting your understanding when you rode him like a stallion and plummeted down on his cock?"

Jessica flushed bright red at the lewd description. Her mind raced to the beginning of their scene. She saw Kade hit the button to turn off the camera and the audio as he told her where the supplies were in the room.

"You don't have to answer that one, Detective. Hope you're strong enough to be an actual Dominant and trample him when it's needed," Cassandra said, pushing off the wall.

"A Dominant need not trample a submissive. They must come willingly with their own power in a submissive state and exchange theirs for the desires of the Dominant to provide mutual benefit and pleasure." Jessica quoted the words from one of Alexandra's manuals.

Cassandra clapped slowly in response.

"Congratulations, Detective. You know the words. Too bad that's not how it works in practice."

With that, Cassandra turned and walked away. As Jessica stood watching her disappear down the hall, she fumed. She was tired of everyone turning their back on her because they didn't think she deserved the respect she was working to earn. Everything in her seethed in anger as she stormed toward the spa.

CHAPTER NINETEEN

Ian's head jerked up from the computer screen on his laptop when Kade stormed through the door.

"Can you believe that woman? Two cracked ribs and she... she..."

"Gave you the best scene of your life?" Ian offered.

"At what cost? Three days of living without being able to come. God-I was like a lust-filled teenager whose libido was in overdrive."

He stormed over to his desk and hit the spacebar on his computer, waking it up. His fingers danced in the one-finger shuffle across the keyboard.

"I believe that was part of the point, and to prove control, of course. I presume you found them in the cellar?"

Kade glared at him, and Ian threw his hands up.

"Slow down. What happened?" Ian asked calmly.

His fingers slammed the keys. Periodically he moved the mouse with a ferocity born out of agitation. When he was satisfied with his task, he turned to Ian.

"She has two cracked ribs. At least based on the way she moves, I think they're cracked and not fully broken. After our scene the other night, she virtually collapsed on me. I thought it was from our amazing scene, but it looks like it was most likely from pain."

Ian took a deep breath and let it out slowly. "You're jumping to conclusions and trying to dismiss your time together so she can't hurt you. Don't do it, man, it's not worth the cost."

Kade ran his hand through his hair.

"Samantha made a comment about the detective being in pain. Why won't she let me fix it?"

"She's a dominant woman in a male-dominated field where many men don't think she belongs. Jessica, I would guess, is very used to fixing things herself or ignoring them. If you want her to come to you, then give her a safe place to let the world go," Ian counseled.

Kade turned and stared out the window. "I can't go through it all again," he murmured.

"She's not Katherine."

Oppressive silence filled the room.

"Out of curiosity, what was important enough for you to break the keyboard to get done?" Ian asked.

He turned his chair to face his friend but didn't meet his eyes. "I was making sure the spa knew she was coming, the appointments were in the best order, and she had the pain medication she needs when she arrives, as well as alerting the masseur of her ribs and ankle."

Ian chuckled. "Looks like turnabout will be fair play."

A confused looked fell over Kade's face.

"I hate to break it to you-"

"Don't. I'm helping her understand the club for the investigation. The mutually beneficial situation is a bonus."

"And denial is a river in Egypt. Come on, let's do rounds. I saw Cassandra down in the lower service hall," Ian said as he stood.

"When?"

"It was what I was watching when you came in."

Kade frowned.

"Was there anyone else in the hallway?"

Ian nodded. "It looked like she was talking to someone, but the cameras weren't angled to see who. Have the command center run the tapes back and we can go do rounds around the club. I think the walk will do you good."

Kade stood up and tapped a couple keys on the keyboard before following Ian out the door.

"Do you have a sit rep from the team?"

"Yeah. Let's walk and talk," he said, heading for the door.

"How's Jillian?"

"Doing better. The situation at the restaurant shook her up, but her memories are coming back, and that is helping the situation."

They walked out of the office and headed to the lower service staircase. Kade's brows pinched in frustration.

"How does she do it?"

"How does she do what?" Ian returned.

"The balance. Strong businesswoman and doctor by day, submissive by night."

Ian chuckled as they headed down the service corridor.

"She's submissive to me, not the rest of the world. I appreciate the fact she trusts me to do things which are horrible out of context and I trust her to be able to communicate what she needs without holding back for fear of my reaction. It's a practice. A constant work in progress. You know this. Hell, you teach it."

Kade let out a strained breath. "I guess that makes me a fraud," he said in resignation.

"No, it means you haven't found a strong enough Dominant," a female voice said from behind them.

Both men turned in unison. Cassandra stepped into view. Her four-inch stiletto heels brought her closer to Kade's height. The body-hugging red dress caressed all her curves in the right places.

"What are you doing down here, Cassandra?" Ian demanded.

"Stand down, Mr. Breckenridge. You're just a security consultant around here," she said, flipping her keycard up between her long fingers. "I was granted access to all areas of the club by Alexandra."

Kade furrowed his brow. He didn't remember such a request hitting his desk, and Alexandra always talked to him about access.

"When? More importantly, why?"

Cassandra shrugged casually and stepped toward Kade until she was inside his personal space.

"I got a note from her office saying she was granting me full access to learn how the club worked," she said as she ran a finger down the front of his shirt. "She did agree to train me as a club Dominant, but then she took off, on vacation or business or whatever is the current excuse."

"Back up, Cassandra. You do not have my permission or the permission of anyone in my realm to touch me."

A lazy smile curled around her lips as she worked her hand lower down his body.

"It's okay, Kade. I know you're showing the detective the ropes around here. Maybe it's to help her department understand us or maybe you think something odd is going on in a SEX club. You know she's just playing at being dominant. I, on the other hand, was hand-picked by Alexandra to be trained as a Dominant."

"This is your last warning," Kade growled.

"Come play with me, Kade," she said as her hand reached for his crotch.

He took a quick step back and Cassandra fell forward. Seconds later, she was kneeling on the floor in front of him, her arms wrenched up behind her back.

"Looks like you need to go back to your lessons, Cassandra. When a person says no, unless otherwise negotiated, they mean it. A good Dominant knows this fact. A club Dominant lives by it. You are neither."

Cassandra's face contorted in pain.

"Let me go," she spat.

"With pleasure," he said, releasing her arms.

Immediately, she fell forward, her hands smacking the tile floor with a resounding thud.

"About that access-consider it revoked. This is your first warning. Security will be advised of your watchlist status," Kade said tersely.

Footsteps reverberated against the wall.

"Mr. Kinkaid, how can I help?" Jason Dean asked as he came into view.

Cassandra glared up at him and scrambled to her feet.

"Please take Cassandra to the Command Center and process her on a level one violation of club protocols," Kade said without lifting his gaze from hers. "Also, take away her status as a club recognized Dominant. She can co-top with the approved members or she can bottom. One of those might bring her some well-needed humility."

KADE MOVED THROUGH THE CORRIDORS.

"Where the hell are we going?" Ian asked from behind him, trying to keep up.

"Alexandra's office."

Minutes later, the pair rounded the corner. Kade often avoided this area of the club, preferring Katie bring him the necessary paperwork rather than reminding himself of his failure.

"Mr. Kinkaid," Katie said in a flustered tone, her fingers hitting the keyboard in a rapid sequence.

When they approached her desk, the screen was blank, the cursor sitting in the log-on button.

"Afternoon, Katie," he said with a smile.

"What brings you here? If you needed files, I can bring them to you," she said, her fingers tapping against the desk.

"Everything okay?"

"Yes, Sir. You startled me is all. I'm not used to you coming down here."

He leaned against her desk, half sitting on the corner.

"I know. I'm sorry. I appreciate your efficiency and focus.

Without you, I'm sure I would have sunk this ship in the first few weeks."

Ian snorted from behind him, and Kade turned to throw him a glare.

"Just doing my job, Mr. Kinkaid. It would piss Alexandra off if she came back to this place in a state of disaster. With my proximity," she said with a shrug, "call it self-protection."

Kade chuckled. "Fair enough."

"Is there something you needed?"

Katie adjusted in her chair and glanced at her watch.

"Am I keeping you from something?"

She stilled at the question and looked up at him. "No, Sir. I find you a little intimidating."

Kade stood up and took a step back. "We've worked together for years. You work directly for Alexandra, and you find ME intimidating?"

"Yes, Sir. I... I... you're taking everything in stride and stepping into roles while still doing your job. And all those... muscles," she said, ending in a whisper.

He shifted uncomfortably at her admission. What the hell was going on here? Women didn't throw themselves at him like this and in a span of an hour there'd been two different versions. He wondered what they would think of him if they saw him at heel behind the detective.

The thought of Jessica made his brain spin. Her strength wasn't a show or a front. It came from a genuine place born of hard lessons and fighting for her place. Too many people thought the way to take a male Dominant down was to flirt with them or physically put them there. Jessica was different. She was like a siren calling to his inner most being. Watching Katie make puppy eyes at him was like the splash of cold water he needed. Now he saw what was right in front of him.

"Please provide me with all the access requests from this office for the past six months," he said firmly.

The internal shift in focus was a relief and gave him a new direction.

"Excuse me, Sir?" Katie stuttered.

"The access reports—past six months."

"Um... Okay, but all the access reports cross your desk. Your office is the only area that can grant club access and keycards."

"Katie," he warned, "please do as I ask."

Her gaze didn't meet his; instead it darted around the desk.

"I can email it to you. When do you need it?"

"Now. I know they are all in the database. I need to see all approvals for the past six months. This isn't a hard request."

"Yes, Sir. I need a few minutes to get them to you."

"Okay. We'll wait inside Alexandra's office."

Kade could swear Katie's face paled at his pronouncement.

"I'm sure you've got better things to do, Sir."

"Nope," he said to Katie, then turned to Ian. "Shall we?"

CHAPTER TWENTY

J essica stared at herself in the mirror. The image staring back at her looked nothing like she'd seen before. Her hair, pulled back in an updo, accentuated her cheekbones while the red lipstick drew the eye straight to it.

She let her gaze drop to the long black palazzo pants which danced around the edge of her four-inch black strappy sandals. She was thankful for the slight platform in the front which gave her the height but relieved much of the pressure from her toes. While her ankle was on the mend, heels were a killer in the best of times.

On top, a white button-down blouse with silver and crystal studs flowed to tight French cuff sleeves held with the cufflinks to match. The masculine style touches complemented the outfit in a perfect juxtaposition of femininity. Around her waist, Samantha was snugging the brocade waist cincher.

"Too much," she said with a grimace.

Behind her, Samantha let out the laces a little and peered over her shoulder.

"Better?"

With a nod and a smile, Samantha's form disappeared back

behind her. Several tugs later, Samantha declared her work to be done and walked around to admire the final look.

"You look breathtaking," Samantha said with a Cheshire grin.

"It's not very... fetish."

"You've looked at too many porn sites. Dominant women don't show up in lingerie, thigh-high boots and a corset-unless they are getting paid or because dressing that way makes them happy. Besides, no one will question your position tonight."

Samantha handed her the club insignia on a silver chain.

For a long moment, Jessica stared at it. She was dominant in every place in her world, but this was one area she felt unprepared. Jessica supposed too many years of being told by her grandmother to be passive in the bedroom were hard to unlearn. Still, she admitted the last scene with Kade felt right. It wasn't as lopsided as she'd thought it would be. The ebb and flow, give and take of it were images which played in her nightly dreams.

"I'm nervous. What if I make a complete fool of myself?"

Samantha smiled. "You won't. It's natural to be nervous. Any Dominant who tells you they weren't nervous the first time they stepped out is lying through their teeth. No one steps into a world which could lead to taking the reins of a relationship without being afraid of failure or making a fool of themselves."

Jessica frowned. "Thanks. Quite the pep talk," she said with a scowl. "Especially since 'the submissive' I'm nervous to see keeps running over me. Can you believe he called the masseuse and told them about my rib and ankle? Does he think I'm incapable of taking care of myself?"

"That's something you'll get used to. Kade wants to serve. To make your life easier, better. It is his way of taking care of you so the world isn't such a burden."

Jessica huffed. "I thought the Dominant was supposed to make all the decisions and carry the weight of the relationship."

"It only looks that way to the uninitiated."

She pulled on the pendant at the end of the chain and stared at the Dominant insignia.

Samantha grasped her shoulders and smiled. "Jessica, I've been at this for a while. I've seen Dominants come and go. You are up there with some of the best I've seen. You care. You're scarily observant of everything around you, and you're patient. It's exactly what Kade needs. He'll push all your buttons because he can, but I know you'll give as good as you get.

"When you leave tonight, you'll have a better handle on our world. It's time to take all that studying and put it to practical use. If you lead, Kade will follow, but you have to let him in so he can serve you."

A shudder passed through her at Samantha's words. The weight of the world felt heavy. Letting someone in required trust. It was a process. She trusted Kade even if she didn't understand why. Did she trust herself not to sabotage the whole thing out of fear?

"What if I muck it up?"

"You will. Things will go sideways. It's part of life. We're a family here. When it all goes wrong, we'll be here to help things get back on track, and when it goes amazing, we'll be here to celebrate."

Jessica took a deep breath and nodded.

"Now, if we are done with the nonsense, there's a party to go to," she said, pulling on the collar of her trench coat.

"What are you wearing to the party?"

Samantha slipped into her heels and grinned over at Jessica.

"A smile."

THEY WALKED BETWEEN THE TWO BUILDINGS, AND JESSICA glanced at the driveway. A line of limousines was stacked end to end from the door to the road. For the first time since she'd taken on the assignment, she wondered if she really were out of her depth in a sea of the upper echelon of the nation's capitol.

"Wow," she mumbled.

Samantha paused and threw her a smile. "You will be great. Breathe. It's a play party-well, somewhere between the event of the quarter and a play party, to be more precise."

"Why do I think you are leaving out a large swath of information?"

She shrugged. "Probably because I am, but then again, was it in my court to inform you or the head of security? Let me think on it."

Jessica scowled at the response. "Spill it, Ms. Kingston," she said authoritatively.

Samantha laughed. "Almost there. A little more practice and even I might fall to my knees for you," she said with a wink.

"In the meantime, tell me what I'm walking into or you'll find me less of an ally in the future."

"Touché, Detective. Well played."

Jessica stopped before they reached the side entrance to the club. "Now, Samantha."

"Ooulı, feisty. I like it," she said and shot Jessica another grin for good measure. "Tonight is the quarterly art showing of Parker Chase."

"Art showing? And you can't mean Parker Chase the art recluse? Why would he do an art showing in a BDSM club? I don't imagine he's doing it for the money."

Samantha nodded. "The same. The rest of the world pays millions for his pieces. Here, women and men beg to become his art installations. This is his outlet. A place where there's less pressure to create what is acceptable to the outside world. He's a genius when it comes to creativity."

A scowl masked Jessica's face. "I'm not following."

"It's simple. He uses the actual human form to create art. The reason the main areas have been closed off for the last couple days is because he likes to work on his shows in private. Hiring the art, interviewing the art, making sure the art is fuckable and will be interactive enough."

Jessica worked to wrap her mind around the words, but little of it made sense to anything she'd ever known.

"Did you say fuckable art?"

"I did."

"How do you fuck art? I mean, don't the nails in the frame leave abrasions?"

This time Samantha stopped, eyed Jessica, and let out a deep laugh.

"Funny. It'll all make sense once we get inside, if I can get you that far," she said, nodding her head toward the door.

Jessica sighed and stepped forward, only to be stopped by Samantha's hand on her arm.

"Don't let anyone give you shit in there. There are people used to getting their own way, but here, it's a different playing field. If you want to play, then negotiate play. If you want to watch, then watch. Should you find it all too overwhelming, there's no shame in bowing out."

"Thanks for the warning, but I've seen some freaky things in my life. I'm sure this will be fine," Jessica said, feigning confidence.

"That's the spirit, Ma'am."

Samantha dropped her eyes to the floor before bringing them up to stare at Jessica with a twinkle of mischief. She took the lead and pushed the door to the club open. The cacophony of sound, music, smells, and formal attire assaulted their senses.

Jessica forced her mouth to stay firmly closed as she looked around the transformed foyer. *It is going be a long night*, she thought to herself.

As they stepped fully into the foyer, Jessica saw a line of people moving through the front door. The men wore anything from a tuxedo to a basic loin cloth while the variety of outfits for the women were long, expensive evening gowns to the same loin cloth as the men.

"Good evening, Samantha," a male voice said to their left.

Beside her, Samantha didn't move, but her eyes dropped to the floor.

"Good evening, Sir," she whispered.

"You are overdressed, my dear."

"As you say."

With nothing further between them, Samantha unbuttoned the trench coat and the man behind slid it down her shoulders. Jessica watched the entire interaction in awe. It was like electricity shot between them, each movement a well-practiced dance. Something in her longed to interact with someone on such a deep level.

With the coat removed, Samantha stood proudly bare in her platform heels, a black loin cloth her only coverage. She was beautiful, and the man beside her beamed with pride.

"Sir, I'd like you to meet Jessica. Jessica, this is Ivan, my Dominant."

"Good to meet you," Ivan said as he stepped around Samantha.

"Likewise. I've heard about your handiwork as of late. Mostly likely well deserved," Jessica said, then flashed a smile at Samantha.

"Indeed. The situations of late cause much stress and someone doesn't handle it well."

"Then it is a good thing she has a village to keep her in the right place."

Ivan chuckled and nodded. "It is true. My pet takes a village to keep her in check," he said and turned to Samantha.

He placed a hand on her back as he stepped to her side. "If you'll excuse us, we have an appointment to keep. I hope you enjoy the art show, Jessica," he said with a deep rumble.

She could see the attraction Samantha found in him.

Without another word, they walked off and disappeared into the crowd.

Jessica turned back toward the vast expanse and let her eyes roam the room. In the center was a woman dressed in a hoop skirt. Around each tier of the skirt a large metal ring held a line of champagne glasses. If she moved, the glasses would topple, but her position made it impossible for her not to engage the crowd as they passed. Beside her, a man dressed in black pants and a white shirt open to his waist offered champagne to the incoming guests. Around both their necks, she spotted the club's submissive insignia. As she approached, the man nodded his head toward her.

"May I supply a beverage for you, Ma'am?"

"You may."

With a slight bow, the man picked up a champagne flute off the skirt, placed his hand under the base and handed it to her so she could pick it up by the stem between her fingers. Each move was precise. Each one efficient but elegant.

Champagne in hand, Jessica moved deeper into the club. Men and women tied in intricate rope harnesses decorated large columns. The artist had replaced the tables beside some of the club chairs with humans on their hands and knees with a serving tray steadied across their back and shoulders.

Large cages hung from the ceiling, each one filled with a person. They had bound some in ribbons, some were dressed in elegant evening gowns with strings of crystals tying them in place, and others were held in place on sticks that disappeared into their bodies. She presumed they vibrated as she watched their forms twitch and wiggle.

Jessica made her way languidly around the room, taking in every form of bondage imaginable on every wall. Bodies of every shape and size were on display, each one decorated to make them spectacular. There was a pride in the work on display. The surrounding crowd ebbed and flowed as the club filled.

"What's tonight's theme, Sir?" she heard a woman ask a man next to her.

"Irresistibly Bound," he replied.

"I can't wait to see what he's done for the interactive exhibits," she said excitedly.

Based on what she could see from the static exhibits, she couldn't imagine what was in store once the main hall doors finally opened.

CHAPTER TWENTY-ONE

K ade watched Jessica move through the club.
"Put your tongue back in your mouth-it's unsightly," Ian joked.

He shot him a playful glare and returned his gaze back to the club. The tight corset accentuated her figure and the white blouse's masculine cut was breathtaking. Everything in him wanted to go to her, but he also wanted her to experience the art show in all of its glory. This was one of the most decadent events the club threw for its members. Alexandra had worked with Parker Chase when she'd first arrived in DC. His proposal for a human art installation had been intriguing. Now it was a mind-bending spectacular.

The week leading up to the event was always stressful, but this time Kade was in the driver's seat. It forced him to rely on the entire team to pull it together, and there were points in the week he wasn't sure it would happen. Now he could sit back and focus on the one distraction which threatened to derail him in more than one way.

"It is quite the spectacle, Parker," Ian said as the artist approached them.

"Wait until you see inside the hall," he replied with a light Italian accent.

"Thank you for your patience this week." Kade nodded.

"It was a pleasure working with you, Mr. Kinkaid. But I must say, I do miss our Alexandra. When is she due to return home?"

The question was on everyone's mind, and Kade still didn't have an answer. Ian's ground team was monitoring, but there'd been no sign of Edmund despite the information they'd obtained earlier in the week.

"You know Alexandra, Parker. She'll return when she decides to return. That woman doesn't submit to the whims of those around her."

Parker let out a soft chuckle. "That is true, my friend. She is most definitely an iron fist in a velvet glove most of the time. Though there's something about her I can never understand."

"Yes. She's an enigma wrapped in a mystery for most of us," Kade acknowledged.

"She'd be a glorious art piece. Maybe I'll put her on a throne atop a crowd. Better yet, I wonder if she'd let me bind her feet underneath a long skirt for fun."

Kade thought about the many sides of the woman in question. Parker was closer than he realized to perfection in his idea.

"If you have a few minutes, there's someone I'd like you to meet," Kade said, avoiding both the confirmation of the idea or the denial of it.

"This is a first, Mr. Kinkaid. You are usually the muscle I want to tie to the wall."

Kade's eyebrow shot up in response, but he said nothing. Instead, he led them through the ebb and flow of the crowd until they got to the other side of the room and stepped behind Jessica without a word.

"You look stunning, Ma'am," he murmured against her ear.

She startled at his unexpected voice.

"Sneaking up on me isn't advisable, Mr. Kinkaid. You may find yourself on the floor in an unsightly display."

"We may have to see that in action at some point, Ma'am," he challenged, the smile evident in his voice. "There's someone to whom I'd like to introduce you."

She turned to face him, and his mouth went dry. From across the room she was stunning. In front of him she made him want to steal her away from the crowds and keep her for himself.

"Jessica, I'd like you to meet Parker Chase. Parker, this is Jessica. She's been working with the security team for the past few weeks," he explained.

Parker took her hand and brought it to his lips, planting a soft kiss on the edge of her knuckles. A sting of jealousy raced along Kade's nerves, but he held his expression in polite reserve.

"You are stunning, Ms. Jessica. Should you ever want to be made into a masterpiece, please let me know," he said, his breath grazing across her skin.

Kade clenched his jaw. He had an animalistic instinct to growl and tell Parker to fuck off, but he knew the man was being polite. His reaction caught him off-guard and he laid a hand on the small of Jessica's back in an innate act of possession.

When Parker released her hand, Jessica looked up at him, the question clear, but it faded as soon as she turned back to Parker. Her face bloomed into a full smile.

"You flatter me, Parker. The human artwork is stunning. I didn't know the human form could be expressed in so many ways."

"Wait until you see the main hall. It is one of my best showings," he said with pride. "Speaking of, I must attend the final preparations. The doors open in forty minutes and this crowd gets restless when the time approaches. I can't leave my adoring public waiting. It was a pleasure to meet you, Jessica."

He bowed with a flourish, turned, and disappeared into the crowd.

As soon as he was gone, Jessica turned to Kade. "Mr. Kinkaid, if you have no immediate concerns, I'd like to see you in a private room below."

The sternness in her voice sent a thrill and a dread running through him.

"Let me check in with Ian and the team, Ma'am. If everything is going smoothly, I'll meet you in the Sapphire Room, if it pleases you."

Jessica nodded and walked off.

"ON YOUR WAY TO AN EXECUTION?" IAN ASKED AS KADE approached the end of the bar.

"To be honest, I'm not entirely sure."

Ian furrowed his brow in disbelief. "I call bullshit, my friend."

"Let's just say, I may have stepped in it with a self-rescuing princess," he said grimly.

"Man, there's your first mistake. Jessica's no princess. That woman's a queen well in control of her kingdom. You'd do well to bend the knee, as they say," Ian said with a snort.

Kade frowned his displeasure.

"Do you have everything covered up here in this madhouse?"

Ian folded his arms over his chest and nodded toward the door.

"Thanks. I owe you one," Kade said, slapping Ian on the shoulder as he walked by.

"Don't thank me yet. You don't know what's in store for you down those stairs."

Ian's words haunted him as he made his way down the stairs. He'd survived bitter realities in hostile war-torn situations. Stared down the most frightening realities of humanity, but the simple walk to a room where a very irritated woman waited for him sent him into cold sweats.

He wanted to delay the inevitable. To slow the walk and hope he could make up an excuse for the reason he'd tarried so long before meeting her, but he knew from experience it was the wrong move.

She might not wield a whip, but he didn't know if her sheer disappointment wouldn't cut deeper.

Kade rounded the corner and took a deep breath. In this room was everything he wanted, much of which exhilarated him with just a touch of fear he couldn't explain. His instincts were one thing; his actions would be another. He lifted his hand and knocked on the door, not daring to barge in on her space again.

"Enter."

He pushed the door open and glanced at the control panel on the wall out of habit.

"Everything is off, Mr. Kinkaid. No one will see our interaction," Jessica said with cold assurance.

She stood in the middle of the room, facing the wall of mirrors as he walked in. Not used to being unsure of himself, he fidgeted and waited for her next move.

"It was my understanding you were a well-trained submissive, at least according to the intel I've gathered over the last week."

"Yes, Ma'am," he replied.

"What are your training and instincts telling you to do right now?"

He shifted his weight uncomfortably from one leg to the other.

"Kneel. But I'm sure you'd want me to ask for forgiveness."

Jessica's eyes narrowed in the mirror's reflection. "The question is why would you ask forgiveness?"

Kade sighed. He guessed at what she wanted him to say. Disappointment slammed through him.

"I presume it would be for my possessive overreaction upstairs."

His answer was clipped. She needed to know he would not step down from a challenge, either from her or anyone else. He wouldn't pretend to be anything other than what he was, and he could be protective, possessive, and loyal to anyone who stepped into this part of his life.

Jessica turned and faced him, and he wondered if she could see into his soul. Everything in him was drawn to her.

"Kade," she breathed. "The real question is why are you so possessive?"

The question stunned Kade, and his head jerked up, his own hard gaze meeting hers.

"Because you're mine," he stated without reservation.

She crossed her arms over her chest and tilted her head to the side. "Is that so? I could swear it is the Dominant who calls the submissive mine."

Kade took a stalking step toward her. "In actuality, I believe it is an inequitable exchange of equals."

Jessica refused to move. "An interesting perspective. Which means, by your own admittance, you enjoy our little game?"

He took several more steps toward her. When he stopped, he watched her crane her neck up to look at him.

"Yes, Ma'am. I am fond of the game, but I'm far fonder of you. Everything in me wants to earn you in every way possible. I want your body until you are squirming under me in delight, pleasure, and ecstasy. I want to know how you see the world and share adventures with you. I want to be the person to which you entrust your deepest secrets."

Kade watched the shallow rise and fall of her chest. He wanted to learn every nuance about her so he could lift her world when it got heavy and take the pain away when she gave it up. The next move was hers. They stood on the precipice of something spectacular, if she would take the leap.

"Then kiss me," she said breathlessly.

The words sang through his body like an electrical current. His brain slid in confusion, not sure the words were actual rather than imagined. Kade lifted his hand and traced the outline of her bottom lip. Her shoulders relaxed as the tension drained from them. He slid his hand across her cheek and cupped her head. A fiery intensity flared in her eyes at his touch.

He lowered his head until they breathed the same air. For a long moment, he held the embrace. Then he kissed her. Her warm lips pressed against his. The potency of her answer surprised him. Her mouth probed and commanded him as she took control of the kiss she'd demanded. Her tongue battled his as she pressed into him. Her hands pressed against his chest. Possession, need, and desire poured from her.

Kade's body responded to her aggressiveness with untamed arousal. His cock throbbed, demanding release. Jessica rotated her body into his, and it took every ounce of restraint not to grab her ass and drag her up his body until he held her in his arms.

"Kneel. You're hurting my neck at this angle," she commanded, breaking off the kiss.

Without hesitation, he fell to his knees. Jessica resumed her onslaught, wrapping a hand in his hair until he growled in pain. Her lips landed on his once again. No longer hesitant, her movements were firm and commanding. When she broke off the kiss, both of them gasped for breath.

"I wonder who is possessive of whom, Ma'am," Kade said with a gasp.

Jessica leaned forward until their foreheads touched.

"I believe it is a matter of a mutual consideration of 'mine.'"

She sucked in a long slow breath above him. The scent of arousal hung in the air between them.

"Yes, Ma'am. So it seems."

He could hear her sharp intake of breath, but she didn't move.

"I don't know this game well, but I don't give up control. Most possessive men want control. They've always wanted to 'protect' me under the guise I am weak, smaller, or lacking in intelligence. Every day I must prove I belong in the line of work I've chosen," she confessed.

Everything in Kade stilled. More than once he'd had those exact thoughts, and each time she'd proven to be far tougher than he'd given her credit for. It was a weakness and one she would demand he break.

171

"I will teach you the steps I know until you find the steps you want to do," he vowed.

Jessica straightened and took a step back. "I believe there's a party to get to, and I've kept you far too long from your duties."

Kade grinned up at her.

"What I hear you saying, Ma'am, is what the hell is fuckable art and can we go see it now that we've got this possessive nonsense out of the way?"

She laughed and signaled him to stand up. "Yeah. How do you make art fuckable? Even Samantha wouldn't tell me that one."

He smiled to let her know he understood the inside joke.

"Let's just say Parker is a perverted artist with a penchant for the more extreme ideas of sex."

Jessica shook her head in frustration. "You're not helping."

Kade offered his arm to her as he turned toward the door.

"It's one of those seeing is believing type things," he said as he led them out of the room.

CHAPTER TWENTY-TWO

They stepped out of the room together. Kade paused and let Jessica step into the lead. He fell in, two steps behind her and to her left. She could see him out of her periphery. Without a word, they moved into the throng of the crowd. There was something comforting about his presence. The way he both commanded a room and gave her deference in the same motion. In every story she'd read, they presented only the extremes. The weak woman bowing before a man or the subservient male bowing before an ice queen, but the reality was nuanced...different.

In front of them, a crowd formed at the main hall's double doors. A twitter of anticipation filled the space. What only a few days ago seemed vast in its emptiness now felt confining. Jessica stopped on the edge of the crowd and waited, observing the actions and reactions of the members.

"Well, well, well," a female voice called from her right as the woman approached. "It looks like someone is pretending to be your submissive because you know nothing about being a real Dominant, or you finally got a clue."

Jessica turned to Cassandra and smiled.

"Jealousy isn't a good look on you," she said confidently.

"And you've found teeth. Well done, Mr. Kinkaid. You are a better trainer than I gave you credit for in my lack of finding a good mentor."

Behind her, Kade didn't move.

"I've always had 'teeth,' as you say. I've learned when they serve me best and when to observe my surroundings. Besides, a teacher is only as good as the student chooses to learn."

Cassandra took a melodramatic step back. "Put a corset on you, Detective, and you think you own the place."

Jessica closed her eyes in irritation and sought her own control.

"First-if you'd read the manual you'd know using my outside title, name, or position is forbidden and a clear violation of club rules and privacy. As we are standing directly in front of the head of security for this club, I'd advise you to watch yourself. Second, you may address me as Jessica or Ma'am, and will do so respectfully."

Cassandra gave a scoffing laugh.

"Why would I address you as Ma'am? Because you wear a Dominant pendant given you without the need to go through any of the testing and programming? Some of us aren't screwing the help to get around the rules."

A smile flickered on the edge of Jessica's mouth as she thought about the grueling hours she'd spent the last few days poring over case notes while passing several club tests to earn the pendant around her neck.

"If you'd focus on studying rather than lurking around the club all day, I am sure you would find the pendant that best suited you too. It just might not be the one you think you deserve."

She watched Cassandra's mouth open then close. A flicker of irritation shone in her eyes. "Maybe I just need a vacation," she huffed. "I hear St. Kitts is beautiful this time of year."

Before Jessica comprehended her statement, Cassandra turned and faded into the crowd.

She pivoted and faced Kade. His hand was on the microphone button of his radio giving orders she couldn't hear.

Jessica opened her mouth to give her own set of commands, but Kade held up a finger. A scowl marred her face at the dismissive gesture, but she paused and waited for him. A range of emotions played across his face. Periodically his finger pressed on the microphone button, and his mouth moved in words she could not hear over the ever-increasing din of excitement. Around them, the crowd pulsated as it moved forward. Patrons set drinks on nearby trays, and a crush of bodies moved around them like a stream around a boulder. Kade did not move; he didn't even notice. Everything in her wanted to demand a radio, but she was a guest to the security. A consultant on a wider case, and even with the coincidence of the word Cassandra used, there was no hard evidence placing her in any part of the case.

She took a deep breath and thought about the case. In her mind, she twisted and pushed each piece of information, but little of it fit neatly together. All things were pointing to Cassandra, but there was something about her demeanor which bothered Jessica. She'd seen it a handful of times in other suspects. A bravado to cover a lack of self-assuredness—or maybe it was exactly what it appeared, and she was overconfident. Frustration welled up in her. She felt helpless to control or solve anything.

"Ma'am," Kade called, his voice full of concern.

Focusing on his voice, Jessica snapped out of her internal thoughts.

"Yes?"

"There you are. Everything okay?"

"That depends on what your team is doing about Cassandra," she replied with irritation.

Kade nodded in understanding. "They are searching for her. With the amount of video and audio surveillance and the extra manpower supplied by your captain, they'll find her soon enough."

Jessica shook with impatience. "Then we'd better get moving.

Two more sets of eyes will make the task go faster. She knows something. We can't let her get away."

In front of her, Kade stood stoically in his place with no sign of movement.

"No, Ma'am," he replied.

"Excuse me?"

"I'm sure my response was clear. With the respect due, there's nothing we can offer to the team. They are on duty. You are not. When they find her, and they will, I've given strict instructions to take her to Interrogation Room One."

She wrinkled her brow at his words.

"Did you say Interrogation Room One, as in this place has more than one interrogation room?"

Kade chuckled at her confusion. "You read the manual, right?"

"Of course."

"Good. The question is how did you miss the interrogation rooms? You caught the medical rooms, wet rooms, and spa rooms, the private ones. Right?"

Jessica bit her lip. In reality, she'd skimmed over the highlights of the club itself. Her sole aim was to pass several certifications to prepare for this evening and not to learn the variations of activities within the club.

"Ah. Someone took a shortcut," he said, shaking his head in disbelief.

"It's been a busy week. I passed all the tests."

"Ma'am, it's not about the test," Kade breathed.

When she heard his words, she looked around the room. The crowd was gone, and only a few stragglers remained.

"Then what is it about?"

"Everything. It's about what makes you think until the emotions carry you into a new realm. Or the place where your body can take the pain until it drains the emotions of their haunting abilities. It is a connection, service, or submission. It is all of those things and none of those things."

Jessica huffed. "Do you always talk in riddles, Mr. Kinkaid?"

"It's not a riddle, Ma'am; it's a path between two or more people." He nodded toward the double doors of the main hall.

"We've got work to do. The art show will wait."

Kade shook his head in fervent disagreement. "No, the team has everything in hand. If they need us, I am reachable. Right now, it is about us, the art and a better understanding... Ma'am."

His big hands engulfed her shoulder and spun her around so fast she closed her eyes to keep her balance. Then his hand ran down her spine and landed at the small of her back. Beside her, he didn't move. His hand did not push, but his desire was clear.

"Do you always top from the bottom?"

"It's a power exchange. We both get input. Besides, Dominants need to learn lessons too."

"You're impossible," she said with a huff.

"Thank you, Ma'am," he said as a slow grin quirked his mouth. "Shall we?"

Jessica nodded her response.

THEY ENTERED THE MAIN HALL, AND JESSICA ALMOST STOPPED dead, except the insistent pressure on her back propelled her forward. Every part of her was overstimulated. The light in the room was subdued with spotlights on framed pieces lining the walls like an art gallery. In the center of the room, two large installations stood under a full array of lights. Each one was surrounded by a crowd of onlookers who gave their own appreciative sounds.

Kade led her through the crowds until they stood in front of the first exhibit. A large golden birdcage hung from the ceiling. The door hung open as if it was falling forward from the hinge. Inside, a naked man stood, his arms and legs bound in loose chains. Upon closer inspection, Jessica noticed the chains weren't attached to anything. She looked down at the placket in front of the exhibit.

Freedom and Bondage

Below the two words were two buttons. One was labeled *Call to Me* and the other *Torture Me*.

Jessica looked up at Kade.

"Press one," he whispered against her ear.

"This makes little sense."

"It makes perfect sense when you let go of what you think you see. Everything about it is art. An expression of the human condition portrayed in the most bawdy way. Press a button."

Nervously she pressed the *Torture Me* button. In the cage, the man writhed. His body pulsed in time with an unseen hand, as he groaned in pleasure. Then it all stopped as quickly as it had started.

"Nice job, Ma'am. You just electrocuted his cock and balls," Kade whispered.

Horror filled her at his words.

Above them, the man in the cage bowed in deference and looked pleased. It was then she noticed the almost invisible pads on his skin and the trail of thin wires going down his legs.

Incongruent emotions flowed through her in a raging torrent. Kade's steady hand once again applied pressure on her back, and they moved toward one of the large installations in the middle of the room. As they approached, she realized there was a woman's body sticking out of what appeared to be a wall. Beside her was a bowl of condoms and dental dams. Jessica watched in fascination as a woman stepped up onto the small platform and grabbed a dental dam. In short order, her skirt was around her waist and she sat down in a slightly reclined position on an odd chair in front of the front half the woman in the wall. When everything was settled, she pressed on the woman in the wall's head until her tongue worked on her pussy. Occasionally the woman in the wall paused or grimaced. The only hint of what she was experiencing came with the occasional sound of a *thwack* which reverberated around the room. Once she processed whatever was happening to her, she returned to her eager focus on the woman in front of her.

"I'm missing something here," Jessica whispered to Kade as she watched the erotic scene in front of her.

Kade nodded and then guided her around to the other side of the wall. There, she saw the other half of the woman's body. Beside it lay a large array of dildos and plugs on one side and on the other, there were canes, floggers, and paddles. On the wall above her was a glove and lube dispenser, along with another bowl of condoms sitting on a shelf hung on the faux wall.

Jessica watched in fascination as a man approached the back half of the body. He picked up a cane and rubbed it against the presented ass. With care, he tapped against the skin in a quick syncopation until it turned pink. Occasionally, he sent the cane through the air with a solid stroke, leaving a bright welt across the skin. She watched the butt cheeks pull together, but the constriction of the wall refused to let the body move more than a breath in any direction.

"What's this one called?" she asked Kade without taking her eyes off the scene playing in front of her.

"*Incongruence*," he replied.

Part of her wanted to look away in horror while it turned another part on in a way she couldn't explain. What would it be like to watch Kade in such a position? To know the pleasure and pain he experienced at the hands of others because of her command? She shook her head at the invading thought. While she enjoyed the art show, there was no way she would allow anyone else to touch Kade that way.

The foreign thought hit her hard and fast. The possessiveness she imagined he'd felt earlier in the evening now washed over her. It wasn't like her, but there was something about it she liked.

CHAPTER TWENTY-THREE

K ade led Jessica to several more art installations throughout the main hall. His eyes were more on her and less on the art. He wanted the overwhelming experience to be enjoyable and constantly watched for any distress or displeasure.

Emotions played across her face as they approached each new piece. He watched in fascination as they rolled through both positive and negative ones only to return to a stone neutral. Jessica might not have a perfect stoic poker face, but the rapid-fire mix of emotional processing left him confused.

They approached the last art piece, and Kade saw Parker watching intently off to the side. He maneuvered them over and turned to see the setup. In front of them, a woman was suspended between two horizontal pipes. Her arms were strapped with thick leather straps to each pipe. The same straps held her legs to vertical pipes holding up the entire structure, placing her body at an L. Sleeves of tattoos wound around her body from her shoulder to the top of the light pink ballet boots encasing her feet at a painful angle. Another pipe rose from the floor, covered in a thick rubber sleeve which was forcing her mouth to open wide in an effective gag while a thick blindfold covered her eyes. On a small frame in front of them was a button and dial.

Bound Pleasure in Pain

A woman walked up to the small set of controls and tapped the button. The hum of a fucking machine greeted the guest. As she turned the dial, the woman in the contraption writhed against the onslaught of the dildo being pushed and pulled into her pussy controlled by the dial.

"I'm not sure if you are an artist or an evil genius," Kade quipped to Parker.

Parker nodded without taking his eyes off the woman struggling in front of him.

"I'm an artist who is also an evil bastard. The two are not mutually exclusive, Mr. Kinkaid," he said as a wry grin pulled on the edges of his mouth.

"Once again, your art show was much anticipated and delivered. Thank you for your patience this week."

Parker turned toward them. "How did you like the show, Jessica?"

Kade watched an unusual blush flush across her cheeks.

"It was beautiful and," she hesitated, "intriguing."

Parker nodded and turned back to watch the bound woman in front of him.

"Interesting descriptions. Both of enjoyment and... disgust is the incorrect word more challenging to your personal preferences."

"Indeed," Jessica acknowledged. "I look forward to the next one."

Parker bowed slightly. "I consider that high praise. I can't wait to hear the new descriptions."

"Mistr... Ma'am," Kade caught himself mid-word and corrected, hoping it went unnoticed.

When Jessica turned and lifted one eyebrow his way, he knew the slip wasn't lost.

"Ma'am," he said then cleared his voice when the sound came out weaker than he intended. "Would you like to adjourn to the bar?"

She remained silent for a long moment. Kade worked to hold his body steady and not fidget as he silently berated himself.

Jessica's eyes didn't move from the watching the woman pull against the bonds in front of them, as the other woman worked the controls to increase and decrease the speed of the machine.

He watched her face for any sign of her thoughts and grew more frustrated with each passing second she refused to reply to the question. Kade took several deep breaths to steady himself. He wasn't some new trainee. He'd served and learned in several difficult environments, but time had a way of softening his skills.

"Yes, Mr. Kinkaid, I would like to adjourn to the bar," she said without looking at him.

Then she turned to Parker and smiled. "Thank you for sharing your art." When the last syllable of the word left her mouth, she took a step toward the door.

Kade drew in a deep breath, placed his hands by his side, and followed her two steps behind her on the left.

THE COMBINATION OF HER ALOOF BEHAVIOR, THE ART SHOW, and their earlier encounter had his entire body throbbing with a pulsating arousal. He was glad the team had found Cassandra. She was in Interrogation Room One but refused to talk. Kade had given orders to go lightly on her and let her stew in the room while observing her. It was an effective technique which often softened a person to talk once their own mind got the better of them.

As they rounded the corner to the bar, Ben Matthews rose from his barstool.

"Well, well, well. Detective Lawson, did you find yourself a cute little submissive male to protect you rather than making the force do it while pretending you are decent at your job?"

Everything in Kade rose in protective anger. The fact someone on her own force believed she was weak and needed constant protection went against everything he'd seen of her over the last week.

"Does no one read the rules to this place?" she huffed and tried to push past the large man.

He watched her arm come up reflexively to cover her ribs and scowled at the unconscious action. There was something he was missing here.

"This is a fucking BDSM club. Who needs rules? You come in here to beat people up or get beat up then get your rocks off and leave," he scoffed.

Kade balled up his hands in anger, but a glance from Jessica and a hand signal to back off left him seething in place.

In front of him, Jessica turned to Ben.

"Detective Matthews, I realize reading is below your comprehension, but it is respectful and basic protocol to know the place you're walking into for work. Next time they provide the materials, it would do you good to read them."

She moved to step around him, but he reached out a hand and grabbed her arm.

"Let go of me."

"Or you'll what?" he sneered.

"Last time we sparred, you ended up losing consciousness if I remember correctly," she said without facing him.

"It was a lucky shot, you little bitch. But if I remember correctly, you came out worse for the wear."

Without another word, he punched her in the ribs. Jessica fell to her knees with a cry of agony. In the time it took him to inhale, Kade knelt beside her. She shook her head and nodded toward Ben Matthews.

When Kade stood he felt a rage of fury that anyone could treat another human being with such disrespect, and it doubled because of his growing feelings for the woman now in agony at his feet.

"Who the fuck on you?" Matthews spat at Kade. "See, boys, she can't even take care of herself in a sex club. Even here a man has her kneeling at his feet."

"You've made a grave mistake, Detective Matthews," Kade replied. His hands clenched and unclenched in anger at his sides.

"And how do you figure that one?"

"First, I'm the head of security here at the club, thus you are my guest. Second, she doesn't need me to fight her fights for her because it sounds like she's already kicked your ass, but I am glad to soften you up for her."

In front of him, Ben Matthews turned pale but refused to move.

Kade pressed the mic on his radio.

"Sec team two, we have a problem in zone 5. I need a guest escort and revocation," he said into the radio without taking his glare off of the man in front of him.

He let go of the button, and a small smile crept across Kade's face. "In case you're wondering, Detective, your captain and I go way back."

Ben glared at him until he was surrounded by three other men with black security T-shirts.

"You can't do this. I'm here on official business."

"No, you were here at the pleasure of the club under a special contract, and now you are not."

When the security team rounded him up and started moving to the front door, Kade relaxed and turned to Jessica. He helped her up from the floor, noticing each wince of pain.

"Jack, I need tonic water with lime," he said as he helped her onto a nearby barstool.

The noise rose with an unexpected suddenness. It was then he realized how big of a scene he'd just made and groaned. Reaching over the bar, he pulled out a small first aid kit and handed Jessica a packet of Ibuprofen.

"You don't need to defend me," she said, her voice barely audible.

"Yes, Ma'am, I do. It is my job here, and for as long as we are in a dynamic relationship, it will be my job. You may tell me not to interfere, as you did tonight, but I reserve the right to override your assessment when it is necessary."

"You're incorrigible," Jessica replied, then tossed back two pain pills with a large sip of tonic water.

"Only to match yours, Ma'am," he said, giving her a mischievous smile.

"Ha. You're always going to be a challenge," she said and shook her head.

The radio popped in Kade's ear, and he prepared for the onslaught of communication about another area in the club. It was a quiet night, and he appreciated the fact everything had gone off without a hitch. There was only one more issue to address, then he could wind this evening down and spend time with Jessica. The thought sent everything in him into overdrive.

"Break. Break. Sec one, Sec one this is Command, over." The voice over the radio pulled his attention at his call sign.

He knew Tanner was running Command and would likely razz him based on the camera feed from the bar, but the forced break in traffic pulled at him.

"Go for Sec one," he said into his mic.

"Sec one, we've got a situation with CO. I need you in command, now. How do you read?"

A scowl marred Kade's face. "Lima Charlie. Wilco. Two mikes out."

"Roger."

Kade turned to Jessica and frowned. "I've got a situation which needs my attention. Can you take over the situation in Interrogation One?"

A smile pulled at the edge of her mouth, and he wanted to laugh.

"With pleasure. Go take care of your problem," she said and picked up her tonic water.

Kade gave her a slight bow and then turned to walk to Command. Everything in his world was lighter than it had been in a long time.

Once they got Atlas back home safe and figured out how to stop Edmund, his world would be on the perfect trajectory.

He pushed the door open and his face fell. Chaos erupted across five screens, and three security personnel were on the phone while Tanner issued orders.

"Sit rep," Kade called over the noise. "What the hell is going on?"

Tanner looked over at him, a phone glued to his ear. Without taking away his gaze, he hit the speaker phone button.

"We've got a mayday from the yacht. The crew is reporting all crew down and an unknown personnel onboard. Current location of Houdini and Princeton are unknown."

"What do you mean, unknown?" Kade growled.

"Sir, we've gotten a mayday call from the crew. That's all we know."

"What the hell is happening down there?"

"We'll have eyes on in five mikes."

Kade wanted to punch something. He never was never helpless when protection was his detail, but in the span of a handful of months all he'd ever felt was helpless, it seemed.

Ian walked through the door in mid-conversation.

"Send the footage to Empyrean Command. We'll have a replacement as soon as possible."

Kade glared at him, waiting for an explanation of the chaos and the lack of information.

Beside him, Ian inhaled deeply.

"We've got drone footage of the boat. The team is less than four mikes out from the boat."

Before he finished his sentence, the drone footage appeared on the large screen on the wall of the command center. A woman huddled over a male form and a large pool of blood spread out from them. Around them the boat was eerily quiet. There were no signs of the crew or anyone else.

"Are they..." Kade refused to finish the sentence.

The woman on the screen moved and then fell forward, covering the man's body with her own.

"We know Houdini is still alive, but we are unsure of anyone else," Ian said quietly.

Kade stared at the scene as the tender approached. Bodies swarmed the deck. In the distance they could see the search light of a helicopter at the edge of the scene. Then it all went black.

"Command, we've got an injured male at the bow of the boat. Immediate evac. All crew is down, eval in progress." The communication cut.

Kade paced the small aisle at the front of the Command Center to bleed off nervous energy.

"What about Alexandra? Is she okay?"

"They'll report when they know. But we both know that no report is good news, most of the time."

It was easier being on the ground in the thick of it. He hated waiting for the word from the ground teams. Each second that ticked by felt like an eternity.

"Command, Houdini is banged up but only minor injuries. Princeton inflight for evac."

"Copy that, ground," Tanner replied to the radio call.

The atmosphere was smothering, but Kade needed to do something.

"Kade," Ian said, laying a hand on his shoulder. "Go get us reinforcements. We need a new crew and Alexandra needs protection."

Finally, he wanted to scream, but he only nodded to Ian and walked out the door.

CHAPTER TWENTY-FOUR

J essica stepped into the observation room and looked through the two-way mirror to watch Cassandra pace the room.

"Impressive set-up," she quipped to Jason Dean.

He turned to her and smiled.

"Sometimes authenticity makes things better," he said with a shrug. "Or so I've been told."

"You don't partake in these... reindeer games?"

He shook his head. "I've not found anything interesting, but there's no hurry. I like the job, it pays well, it can entertain. Besides, I'll either find my path in this lifestyle or will forever be a vanilla."

She nodded, understanding how he felt. "Tell me what we're looking at here," she said, nodding toward the glass.

"We picked her up in the foyer. I'm told she made a comment about St. Kitts and it sent the team into a frenzy. She's been in the box for a little over ninety minutes, and she's getting really unhappy. No one's been in to see her, although a Detective Matthews tried to bully his way in a bit ago. I told him I was under strict orders to only let you interrogate her."

Jessica sighed. The altercation at the bar made more sense, not that Detective Matthews needed a reason to go after her. He wasn't quiet about his thoughts on women in the police force or their ability to do the job. She thought about filing a complaint to HR, but her previous experience with harassment complaints in the military had left a sour taste and one she'd avoid at most costs. Misogyny was part of the job. She wished it was different, but it was part of working in a male-dominated situation.

"Do you have a file folder with some papers?"

He searched through the cabinets in the room. A few minutes later, he returned with a file folder stuffed with blank paper and two pages which looked like data analysis on top. A pen was clipped neatly on the right edge of the folder, and she smiled at the detail.

"Really? This place even has fake analysis records?" she asked, staring down at the pages inside the folder.

"Yes. So it seems. They are very accurate in their presentation around here, I'm finding out."

"Scarily so," she quipped and walked to the door. "Looks like it's show time. Too bad none of this is admissible."

"Then why do it here and not just arrest her?" Jason asked before she pulled the door closed.

"Because I don't really have any evidence against her. It's only an intuitive feeling, and those won't hold up in court."

Jessica closed the observation room door behind her and approached the interrogation room. Adrenaline pumped through her veins. There was something about these situations which always caused a narrowing of her focus. She straightened, pulled the pen off the folder, and pushed the door open.

"Good evening, Cassandra," she said confidently as she entered the interrogation room.

"What the hell is going on here?" Cassandra growled at her.

"Let's have a seat and see if we can straighten this mess out, shall we?" she replied, pointing to the seat across from her as she approached the table on the side closest to the two-way mirror.

"You've kept me in this room forever. You can't do this. I've got rights. This is kidnapping."

Jessica pulled the chair out from under the table and sat down while Cassandra ranted. She opened the folder and stared at the false data sheet on top.

In any other situation she'd be correct, but the general liability waiver for the club covered situations which fell under edge or intensified play. She wasn't working in an official capacity because she had nothing on Cassandra. Jessica knew it was a gray area.

"Sit down so we can straighten this out in no time. Then we can both get on with our evenings," Jessica said coolly.

Cassandra towered over her in an attempt to intimidate.

"I should inform you that there are a half a dozen observers on the other side of the mirror. Continue this behavior, and I'm sure they'd love to take this to the next level with some handcuffs," she said without taking her eyes off the papers in the folder.

Jessica watched Cassandra continue to pace from the periphery of her gaze, but she refused to look up from the papers. Periodically she'd lift the pen and take a note, then lift the folder and sigh at the pages. After more than five minutes, Cassandra pulled out the chair and sat down at the table as she tried to peer at the papers in front of her. On cue, she shut the folder and looked up, shaking her head.

"There have been several incidents at the club recently. According to the security cameras and other evidence, you are the lead suspect in all of it," she said calmly.

Across the table, Cassandra visibly paled.

"I'm sure there's a reasonable explanation for it. Care to tell me about your connection to St. Kitts?"

"I... I..." she stuttered and stared down at her hands. "I was told to say it to you. That you would know what it meant."

Jessica nodded. "Okay. So there's someone giving you information, who is responsible and involved in these incidents. Why don't you give me a name and we'll clear this all up?"

Cassandra shook her head.

"I understand. With this level of evidence, I don't see anyone else involved. This should be an open and shut case. I'll refer it to another detective in my department. Let me step out and make a couple phone calls to get you transferred down to the station," Jessica said, shifting in her chair in a move to make it look like she would stand.

"Wait."

"Unless you've got something for me, Cassandra, I don't have time to continue to play your games. The club's been collecting video of your movements, and I have a report of your keycard swipes. These place you in several compromised situations. It also violates a number of member rules. With the clientele around here, I can only imagine what they'll do when they hear of a breach this significant."

"It was just supposed to scare them," she whispered, not looking up from the table.

"For what purpose?"

"I don't know. I was... he'll know. I can't."

"Who will know?"

"He's got ears everywhere. Nothing gets past him."

"No one but the Command Center and the people behind the mirror can hear anything."

Cassandra shook her head as tears flowed down her face. Streaks of dark mascara formed black rivers until they dropped off her chin and splattered on the stainless steel table.

"He's always listening. He knows everything," she said, wiping at her face with the back of her hand.

"Here's how I see it, Cassandra. You tell me which one's right. You came into this club to get close to the club owner and worked to scare her by making her think someone else was involved. Or—" She paused. The pieces of the case flew through her. This wasn't making sense. She knew Edmund was involved but couldn't connect Cassandra's involvement. "Someone else put you up to this and is making you do it."

Terror lit up in Cassandra's eyes, and she looked around the room. Without a word she put her hand up and moved it like she was writing on a piece of paper.

Jessica pulled the last page out of the folder. Without taking her gaze off Cassandra, she passed the blank page and pen over to the woman, who was now visibly shaking in her seat.

Cassandra took the paper and pen without a word. She forced her hand to move unevenly across the table, periodically stopping to wipe the tears from her eyes. Jessica tried to read the words upside down but gave up. Pushing the chair back, she stood and paced the small room. She grabbed the folder and opened the door. Jason met her as she stepped out of the room.

"Impressive work, Detective," he said, handing her a bottle of water.

Jessica shook her head in frustration.

"Something's not right. That was too easy," she said, leaning against the wall and taking a long pull of water.

"She's guilty. How hard can it be? It goes like that on TV all the time. Bad guy gets caught, cop pushes, the person confesses."

She sighed. Too many people thought it was that easy. Find the bad guy. Make them sweat a little and poof-confession. Most of the time it was hours, multiple personnel, and a few different techniques to make the suspect crack. That's if you could get them to talk before asking for their lawyer. This one, this one was just too easy.

"Get me a bottle of water for Cassandra."

Jason turned, disappeared into the observation room, and returned with another bottle of water.

"Maybe you're due for an easy one," Jason said with a smile.

"It's not admissible even if it is easy. Ultimately, this is just pretend."

"That's some pretty intense pretend."

Jessica nodded.

"And to think, some people do this for 'fun.'"

She smiled at him and pushed the door open.

At the table, Cassandra fidgeted with the pen. Jessica set the water down on the table beside her, and she pushed the paper toward her in return.

Jessica picked it up and read it. The more she read, the more her brow furrowed. Without a word, she lifted a brow at Cassandra, who returned it with a simple nod.

"Shit," she said and pulled the door open hard.

Ensuring the door shut behind her, she called out to Jason. "Don't you dare take your eyes off of her and don't let her out of that room!"

She wanted to run to Kade's office but knew it would cause too many questions and rumors. With determined dignity, she folded the paper and focused on her destination.

"JOHN, I NEED YOU ON THAT BOAT," KADE SAID INTO THE PHONE as Jessica walked into his office.

He held up one finger at the impatient expression he knew she wore.

"She's everything. Whatever it takes to protect her and don't let her out of your sight. She smart, but there are moments she's irrational."

The silence hung heavy in the room while Kade listened to the conversation. Jessica shifted her weight between her feet. The outfit that was perfect earlier now felt confining.

"Okay. Whatever it takes. Let me know the minute you are aboard. I owe you one, man," he said with a heavy sigh.

Kade punched the screen of his phone with his thumb and ran his other hand through his hair. He closed his eyes for a long minute, then looked up at her. Pain, frustration, and anger mixed in a cataclysm of emotions on his beautiful face.

"How'd the..." He stopped as soon as she shook her head vehemently no.

"Based on that conversation, I take it I'm missing something. We'll talk about it later, whatever it is. Are you done with everything?"

He nodded as his fists pounded hard against the desk.

"Mr. Kinkaid, you look frustrated. I've only got one question for you," she said with a calm, seductive tone.

"What's the question, Detective?" he asked cautiously. His face registered the hesitation that was clear in his posture.

"Punch or fuck?"

If the situation were less dire, she was sure his answer would be immediate, but the question caused a mass of confusion, and she smiled as she watched him become unbalanced. There were two ways to drop adrenaline fast, for most of the men she'd known in the past. Either they wanted to punch something until it, or they, were dead or they wanted to fuck-hard.

"I don't understand."

"Yes you do. It's a simple question. Do you want to punch something and fight it out or do you want to fuck?"

She wanted to laugh, but the information she'd obtained required him to have a clarity he wasn't likely to get to in his current state.

"Fuck."

"Done. Let's take this back to the apartment over the PR firm. The rules are simple. There aren't any. Sometimes a hard fuck is good for everyone involved," she said, pivoting on her heel and heading out the door.

She'd counted to three when she heard the click of his shoes following in her wake. This was going to go exactly like the vague plan in her head or it was a disaster in the making. Either way, the release would do them both good, and they could get back to work.

CHAPTER TWENTY-FIVE

He stared at her retreating form. His brain refused to accept what she'd asked, but his entire being followed her of its own accord. As they wound their way through the club, several people tried to stop him, but he waved them off. There were only two things on his mind: first he would fuck the living daylights out of the woman who'd thrown down the gauntlet to him, and second he would do whatever it took to make sure Alexandra was safe. Guilt gnawed at him for his inability to keep Alexandra directly safe, but his cock only wanted to stress relief buried deep inside of Jessica.

When she stopped at the PR firm's door to unlock it, he invaded her space.

"You better have meant what you said back there," he growled against her ear.

"My only concern is if you are up to the challenge," she shot back, pushing the door open, making him stumble forward.

"You are fucking mine," he said as he followed her up the apartment stairs.

She pivoted to face him as he stepped on the last stair.

"Correction, you are mine. Activity does not equal a change in dynamic. If you think it does, then you need to go find a punching bag. Fucking me hard and fast without rules or dynamics to get in the way changes nothing else between us. Are we clear, Mr. Kinkaid?" she said with a glare.

"Crystal, Ma'am," he growled back.

"Good. I know there are condoms and lube in the drawer by the bed."

Without another word, she turned and walked off toward the bedroom. His hand twitched with the desire to wrap itself in her hair as he buried his cock to the hilt. She was right about one thing: the activity didn't change the dynamic, and it also didn't change how much he wanted to fuck her ruthlessly either.

Jessica was working the last clasps of the corset as he entered the room. When it fell away, he gasped at the outline of her breasts pushing against the white fabric. Her fingers worked down the studs of the shirt in a slow, sensually painful pace until he wanted to demand she hurry. Instead, he balled his fists and forced the impatience back down.

Her pert, tight nipples strained against the fabric. His tongue raced across his lips in a Pavlovian response. The torture continued as she worked the front of her tight black pants. Kade closed his eyes briefly to regulate his rising desires. When he opened them, he walked to the bedside table and ripped open the drawer, grabbing a handful of condoms and lube and throwing them on the bed.

Kade turned back to the bed to see Jessica sitting on the edge. The white blouse hung open as it covered her naked form underneath.

"Fuck me, Mr. Kinkaid. Hard," she said, almost inaudibly.

"With pleasure, Ma'am."

He shoved his pants open and ripped off the edge of the condom foil like a savage ready to conquer. In quick order he covered his aching cock, never so glad he'd gone commando. Kade walked over to Jessica, shoving his fingers into her hair until it wound around his fist. He tightened his hand in her hair and growled at her.

Kade nuzzled against her ear and heard her sigh in response. His lips moved softly against her cheek until he found the edge of her mouth. The minute his lips brushed against hers, she opened to him. He dominated the kiss, using the hand in her hair to move her the way he wanted. Against his body, she was petite and small like a prey to his predatory need.

"Bend over the bed. Now," he demanded.

Her body moved before him, the hand in her hair adjusting her like a rein. Kade grabbed the lube bottle and squirted a large drop of lube on his pulsating cock. Then he ran his hand between her pussy lips and groaned at her tight warmth.

"Let me show you what is yours, Ma'am," he growled as he impaled her with his cock.

Her own slickness added to the lube as his cock invaded her. Below him Jessica spread her legs wide, giving him all the permission he needed.

Kade ground his hips against her ass, then reared back and thrust back into her. Over and over he pushed himself harder. He raised his hand and slapped against her ass, leaving his handprint. It was the perfect combination release of fucking and a slap rather than a punch. Heat and pleasure flooded through him until his thoughts were obliterated in animalistic need. Jessica's muscles clamped down on him as she raced toward her own orgasm. Bending his head to her shoulder, he paused his movements to kiss and lick against her skin. Her shoulder moved in rhythm under his lips as her fingers drove her toward her own release.

"Either fuck me or go away." She hissed her frustration.

"Oh, I plan to fuck you until you can't think, Detective. Right after I make you mine, too."

His teeth grazed across her skin as he bit into her shoulder. Under him she let out a scream of agony which turned to pure pleasure as soon as he released her and pumped into her hard once more. He smiled at the red mark he'd made on her shoulder.

"That's it," she encouraged breathlessly.

Kade widened his stance. His head fell forward as he moaned his reply. He fisted his hand in her hair, pulling it back until her body arched toward him. With a hard slap on her ass, he grunted his response as he firmly wrapped his fingers around her hip. He looked down at her body impaled on his hammering cock. She cried out her approval repeatedly as she rubbed her clit in time with him.

The clenching of her pussy told him she was sitting right on the edge of her own orgasm. Kade brutally slapped against her ass and a scream tore from Jessica's throat as she cried out in release. Jessica slammed her body back into his as they both thrust in a desperate rhythm.

Kade focused on his own sweet pleasure as he relentlessly hammered into her. His punishing thrusts slammed into her as his own pleasure sat right on the edge, refusing his need. He moved his hand and ran a thumb across the tight bud of her asshole.

"I want to take you right here too, at some point," he said as his thumb pressed against the tight pucker.

Jessica moaned. "Only if I can return the favor," she hissed as the last licks of her orgasm spread through her.

"Yes, Ma'am."

The words ignited the last vestiges of Jessica's orgasm and lit the fuse to the next one, sending her pussy into another hard spasm of pleasure. It was all Kade needed to give in to his own demanding pleasure and sent a rush of pleasure exploding through him.

He heard his animalistic growl bounce loudly off the walls as his body jerked and spasmed through every ounce of ecstasy. His breath came in labored pants as he released Jessica's hair and fell forward. Nothing in him wanted to move from the warm embrace of her pussy around his cock. Everything about her was like home. This was what it felt like for everything to be right in the world.

Keeping his thighs pressed into hers, Kade lowered them both to the mattress. His cock twitched as it softened. He wanted nothing more than to stay here, wrapped around her, until he was once again hard. The thought made him smile as he bent his head down and kissed the top of her head. There was so much ahead of them to get done. For the first time in far too long, he felt a unique clarity.

"Better, Mr. Kinkaid?" she asked as she shifted next to him, dislodging his cock from her soaked pussy.

"Much, Detective."

"Then let's get back to work. There are people who need our focus."

Kade wrapped his arms around her and held her tight.

"I'll be right beside you when we arc done, Mr. Kinkaid," she said as if to answer his unspoken question.

He held her for a few more minutes before releasing her and sitting up on the edge of the bed.

"We'll figure it out. I only suggested this to release your pent-up frustration and energy. Not angry sex, not make-up sex, more frustrated *can I punch a wall without breaking my hand* sex," she said, laying a hand on his shoulder.

"You're a unique woman," he replied softly.

"It's more an understanding of men in times of stress," she acknowledged, standing up and walking over to the set of clothes that had been provided to her earlier in the week. She picked out a pair of dress pants and a simple button-down blouse. Kade watched her walk into the bathroom and push the door, but it barely moved.

"Is this your normal avenue of release?"

"Not even close." Her tone was cutting and soft.

"I meant no offense."

He heard the water run and the shuffling of movement. A couple minutes later she emerged, dressed. Her hair was brushed out and placed in a messy bun at the nape of her neck.

"You might not have meant to offend, Mr. Kinkaid, but your question says it scares you that there's nothing here more than me offering you a body to relieve yourself into. I can assure you it is nowhere near the case. However, the next time you want to mark me as yours," she said, her tone deadly serious as she stepped in front of him, "you better be prepared for me to return the favor in any way I desire."

He started to object but stopped when she held up a finger.

"This was a no rules situation. One which I enjoyed a great deal. But all actions have consequences," she said with a smirk. "Now get dressed. And in case you were unclear, that was an order."

Kade relaxed under her gaze and smiled. "Yes, Ma'am."

He walked to the bathroom and cleaned up. As he emerged, he hit the power button on the radio. A dissonant set of voices clattered against his earpiece.

"Does anyone have eyes on Sec one?" a male voice demanded.

"No one has seen Sec one in the last thirty mikes."

"This is the Command Center, find him."

The radio popped and cracked as other voices pushed through the communication line.

Kade took a deep breath into the pleasure which still hummed through his body and prepared for a hard shift back into the chaos.

"Command, this is Sec one," he replied into this radio mic.

"Where the fuck have you been, Sec one?" Tanner screamed.

"Exactly," he hissed. "Offline. Getting clarity."

The radio went silent as he replied.

"Princeton is down hard. The new crew arrival in two hours. Houdini not answering."

"I am Oscar Mike. Be there in 10 mikes."

"Copy that, Sec one."

He ran a hand through his hair. Kade wasn't sure if the relief fuck was well timed or just another hard suffering transition. He was still lost in his thoughts when he entered the apartment's kitchen.

"Heads up," Jessica called from the refrigerator as she tossed him a bottle of water.

He barely looked up in time to catch and fumbled it onto the counter. She was frowning when he picked up the water bottle and glanced in her direction.

"Well, it looks like I wasted my efforts," she said with dismay.

Kade shook his head. "Never wasted. Everyone was looking for me when I turned on my radio. I'd call it ill-timed and well-needed."

Jessica nodded in understanding. "An oxymoron as always," she said and shifted on her feet. "Before we go back, I was on my way to your office from my discussion with Cassandra when the need for this detour became apparent."

Kade perked up and waited for her to continue.

"Cassandra wrote out a confession, of sorts."

He scowled at her. "How does one sort of confess? Doesn't a person either confess or declare their innocence?"

Jessica nodded her head back and forth while her hands rotated in a signal of it not being so simple in real life. "She confessed to doing a number of things, including the knife in the door."

"Perfect," Kade interrupted her. "You go arrest her for harassment and whatever else you can think of and..."

"Not so fast, Mr. Kinkaid. She was being coerced. Cassandra is in a large amount of medical debt after her mother died from several years of battling cancer. She thought she was taking on a job as an undercover reporter. Her contact told her about the Dominant mentor program with Alexandra and gave her all the right words and descriptions to say in the interviews."

Kade blew out a hard breath. The world he'd envisioned as horrible went to horrid the more Jessica talked.

"Cassandra admits putting the knife in the door, but only because her contact threatened to expose her to every member in the club."

He scowled. It made little sense. There were only two sources of membership information kept anywhere in the club archives, and a significant amount of protocols protected those data points.

"She also said the club had an infestation both in the software and the hardware."

"Shit," Kade said blowing out a hard breath.

"My thoughts exactly."

He let the information settle into his thoughts.

"Sec one, this is Command. What's your twenty?"

"Oscar Mike. Got delayed."

"Copy that," the voice replied.

"Jessica, Alexandra was on a yacht in St. Kitts. It was overtaken this evening. When you walked in, I was finalizing the replacement crew. We don't know how bad it is, and I need to get to the Command Center."

She rounded the corner of the island with a stern look.

"Why the hell didn't you tell me? I would have never—" she yelled but stopped when his finger pressed against her lips.

"Because I needed this. It released every emotion that was driving me. You gave me a clarity I can now apply. And you brought me information I needed. Thank you."

Jessica nodded. "What should we do about Cassandra?"

Kade gave her a half grin.

"Leave her in the box for a bit to stew. She's out of the way, and it'll give us time to think of the most appropriate punishment."

Jessica chuckled.

"Now, let's get the rest of this mess sorted out," he said as he headed toward the door.

"On your six," she replied from behind him.

CHAPTER TWENTY-SIX

J essica followed Kade back through the club and into the chaotic Command Center. The minute they entered, Tanner eyed her and quirked an eyebrow. She refused to return anything to him and left her face expressionless as he started the sit rep with Kade. Years of military training had taught her the discipline to know when to jump in the middle of a situation and the time to observe it. In this case, no matter how much it was affecting Kade, the latter was in play.

She moved to the corner of the tight room and watched the images from the large screens change in their perspective. Everyone was on a phone or a radio, and she worked to keep up with the ever-evolving situation playing out in front of her. A scowl marked Kade's face as he caught up on the details, but there was nothing she could do to help.

"Call the boat. Get me Alexandra," he demanded to the room.

"Yes, Sir."

"Where's the team now?"

"The locals are aboard. John is an hour out. The rest are two hours out."

She watched Kade nod his response.

Questions from the case spun in her head. How was the boat situation connected to the knife which connected to Cassandra? What was the motive behind the attack? Was it meant to be an attack? The last one seemed the easiest to answer based on the limited information she'd received. The boat attack was premeditated. The biggest problem was why? There wasn't a clear-cut motivation here. In its simplest form, it sounded like an easy case of a jilted lover, but in this world nothing was ever easy. It was a lesson she'd learned quickly in her immersive time at the club. Things on the surface did not always lead to the motives underneath, and the motives underneath and action did not always synchronize with the visible actions.

She closed her eyes and let the pieces form in her mind, working each one like a puzzle piece. Alexandra and Edmund were in a pro Dominant relationship. For years it was stable, then suddenly he wanted to marry her and stalked her. Now she was on the run and someone had attacked her safe house on a yacht. Then there was the threatening knife in the door and the inference of issues in the club's systems. Jessica's mind dug for the motive. There was a connection to all the pieces, but it felt disjointed, like there was more than one situation colliding at once.

"Detective," a male voice called for her.

Her face pinched in aggravation as the puzzle pieces evaporated, and she opened her eyes.

"Yes?" she replied, working to even out the annoyance from her tone.

"Mr. Breckenridge would like to talk to you," he said.

"About?"

"He didn't give me details, Ma'am. He only asked that I find you."

Jessica nodded and exhaled her frustration. "Lead the way."

"This way please, Ma'am. He's in Mr. Kinkaid's office."

She followed the man out of the Command Center and over to the office. Inside, Ian Breckenridge sat on the couch, his cell phone up to his ear as he motioned them inside.

Without hesitation, Jessica walked over to the large chair in the seating area and took a seat. She watched Ian nod and heard the door of the office close.

"Okay. This whole thing is a cluster. We're missing something. Keep digging," he said into the phone and clicked it closed.

"A flip phone. Interesting," Jessica quipped when he looked in her direction.

"Encrypted. Simple. Comparatively secure," he replied.

Jessica nodded. Technology moved so fast the security of it often lagged far behind the capabilities.

"You 'summoned' me, Mr. Breckenridge?"

"It was more of a request for your help," he replied, a smile pulling at the edge of his mouth.

"So someone lost the request in translation, is your assertion, I am to presume."

"Something like that," he said with a nod. "I like your bluntness, Detective."

"That's new. It rubs most people the wrong way."

"I'm sure. Most people aren't confident enough to put away their preconceived biases."

"And you are?" she challenged.

"I'm fallible, but I try. Which is why I wanted to talk to you. We've got a problem on our hands, and our mutual friend will drown if we don't do everything we can to help him."

"I am sure Mr. Kinkaid is quite capable of bringing this situation to a close. He's well in command of his team and brings in the necessary consults to give different perspectives," she said, pinching her face in a protective glare.

Ian threw up his hands in defense. "It's not a doubt of his skill. Kade and I go back a long way, and that man saved my ass on more than one occasion. I literally owe him my life. But the situation is complicated, and anyone would drown in it. Couple that with his personal relationship with the victim, and he's a bit over his head."

SAPPHARIA MAYER

Jessica sat and watched him without a word. She pulled Cassandra's confession from her pocket and passed it over to Ian.

He unfolded it and read it. Jessica leaned back in the chair and watched his expression change as he made his way down the page.

"Did you tell Kade?"

"The highlights only," she confirmed.

"Where's Cassandra now?"

"Interrogation One."

Ian nodded. She watched as he calculated his next move, but his expression remained stern.

"Okay. I'll get her moved to more pleasant overnight accommodations."

The shift in his voice indicated an undertone of sarcasm, but Jessica had learned not to take much at face value in this place.

"Thank you for trusting me with this information," he said with a nod. "May I keep it?"

"Yes. I've already created what I needed from it."

Ian placed the paper into his inside jacket pocket and pulled out another paper.

"This is the reason I wanted to talk to you," he said, laying the paper on the table and pushing it toward her.

Jessica picked it up, unfolding it and reading the information. It was her turn to school her features as she processed the words.

"This is a very generous offer, Mr. Breckenridge, but I have a job," she said without taking her eyes off the paper in her hand. There were more zeros at the end of the number than she would see if she made captain.

"I am aware. Your talents are being wasted in a constant testosterone contest, if the display at the club's bar was any indication."

Her head shot up, and she glared at him.

"I don't need a white knight trying to save me from the world. I've worked my ass off to earn respect," she spat back at him.

"And yet it still doesn't come to you. This isn't a pity offer, Detec-

208

tive. I am always looking for extraordinary talent to join my team. You have a unique perspective on the world. It's not all gray, and it's not all black and white. From your performance here, you let little get in the way, but you also don't charge into an unknown situation to be the hero. Some of my team could use more of that type of training," he said.

"What exactly is the position, Mr. Breckenridge?"

"Investigations. There will be times when you may need to be a body double or a bodyguard, but those will be rare," he replied, a slight pause stammering his words.

"Because of my... stature?"

Ian chuckled. "We rarely have clients who fit your profile. Though I fully believe you have the skills if necessary. However, I do have a friend with several 'identities' who could use another person on her side when necessary, without blowing her cover."

Jessica looked back down at the paper. She'd always heard about defining moments. This wasn't how she pictured them and yet she sat right on the cusp.

"How soon do you need an answer?"

"No more than three days. My team's workload is exploding. Business is good," he said with an odd sadness.

She nodded. It was always a difficult position for those in law enforcement and security. When it was quiet there was either a storm on the horizon or boredom, but when business was booming, it was easy to be overwhelmed with the constant battles. Ian was offering her the opportunity to pick the battles. She was only hoping it wasn't moving from the flames of a simple fire to the inferno of hell.

"When would you like me to start?"

A smile of relief spread across Ian's face.

"Three weeks. The captain would kill me if I tried to take you away too soon, and I need his help too often to make an enemy."

Jessica sighed and let out an ironic laugh. "Politics to the left of me, blood suckers to the right."

Ian nodded. "It will only get worse from here. Welcome to Breckenridge Security, Ms. Lawson."

Her nose wrinkled in disgust. Never in her career was she subjected to the odd title phrasing given to females. It was always her last name or her title.

"Was it something I said?" Ian asked with concern.

"Other than Ma'am, I'm rarely referred to with a female title. It sounds odd, like someone is guessing at my marital status," she replied.

Jessica shifted in her seat. She rarely voiced her own thoughts on the matter, and being in a male driven industry, rarely needed to deal with it.

"Ah. I understand. Do you prefer Jessica or Lawson?"

"Lawson is fine."

Ian nodded as he stood.

"Then welcome to the team, Lawson. I expect great things from you. For now, I need to go make accommodations for our unexpected guest."

Jessica rose to her feet and reached out her hand. "Thank you."

Ian took her small hand in his and shook it. "Don't thank me yet and don't curse me when it gets hard."

"Noted," she said with a smile and watched him walk out of the office.

HER MIND WAS A CONSTANT DISSONANCE OF IDEAS, information, and thoughts. The earlier fuck with Kade provided clarity to their relationship and the murky waters of working together. On the other hand, the case refused to form any clear motive. She walked over to the long white board, which dominated a small alcove in Kade's office, and picked up a marker. Without thought, she let her hand move across the board. Each stroke of the marker dumped information. None of the ideas connected and she let the free flow of her hand write out the clutter of her mind.

Everything around her grew silent as she focused on the board in front of her. Here, time didn't exist. She marked Edmund as her lead suspect to connect the rest of situations together. Edmund was involved in stalking Alexandra, but was he also the anonymous person behind Cassandra's original assignment? Jessica drew a circle around Cassandra's name with a question mark at the edge. She knew Edmund was fiscally capable of a pursuit, but the motivation was unclear. Above his name she placed the three most likely ones: greed, power, sexual control. Based on her information, she boxed in power and sexual control, though she admitted that the sexual control seemed out of bounds based on their previous professional relationship.

She abandoned her path on Edmund and moved over to Cassandra. Someone had given her an assignment and wanted her to do an exposé on the club owner. But they had also given her information on St. Kitts.

Jessica followed the St. Kitts lead down the board. She listed off the number of people who knew the location as a safe house. Then she listed their locations. Her brow wrinkled in confusion. What was it that Cassandra said in the room? "He's always listening. He knows everything." She wrote the words beside the St. Kitts. How does someone always listen and know everything?

The question twisted in her mind. Her hand worked the marker across the board in an odd stream of consciousness as she word-associated conversation, telephone, conference call, smart phones, bugs. When the last word completed, her whole body stopped. She pulled her phone from her pocket and scrolled through the written confession. Cassandra had written that she thought the club had an infestation in the hardware and software based on her investigation.

She placed a red line between bug and infestation. How would someone bug a place as secure as the club? They logged every single badge in or out. The club assigned each member an individual pin, and their guests screened with a background check. Yet they'd missed something. She stared at the board. Her fingers continued to move between the word bug and St. Kitts.

The office door opened, and the voice barely penetrated her focus.

"Atlas, oh thank God! Are you okay?" Kade's voice rushed as he walked into the room.

"Oh." She heard him pause the conversation.

There was a long pause, and she put down the marker to turn toward his voice.

"I just got word Reece is being airlifted to Miami," he said into the phone he held at his ear. "According to my sources, the object missed his artery by a quarter of an inch. The application of pressure and a move to the recovery position saved his life. The jet will be on the tarmac for your arrival in four hours. Based on the information from my team, it will take you six hours to get back to port. Everything you need will be on the plane when you dock. Wheels will be up as soon as you are ready. We could get you back faster, but I think it is best to leave you on the yacht. A new crew will be aboard shortly to bring her home. Everyone on the new crew I know personally. They were in the general area at the time I put out the emergency call and are en route to you. We are still assessing how this happened."

A scowl marred Kade's face as he walked to the window.

"Excuse me, Ma'am?" he asked the person on the phone in clear confusion.

"I see," he replied. "We'll get this bastard."

The person on the other end asked a question which caused obvious concern.

"We are still trying to locate him, Ma'am." Kade shook his head as he replied. "We don't know."

Kade finished the conversation and turned toward Jessica.

His eyes swept across the board as she watched him take in the mass stream of consciousness.

"You don't think..." he said with a pause and stepped toward the white board.

He shook his head as he looked at the board.

Jessica followed his gaze and the red lines she'd drawn.

"Yes, I guess I do."

"Shit," Kade swore and picked up his phone. "Ian, I need you in my office, now!"

CHAPTER TWENTY-SEVEN

K ade paced his office as he worked through the information on the board. Dominick was missing, they needed to sweep for bugs, Reece had been stabbed, and Atlas was on her way back to DC. He glanced at the motivations Jessica had written over Edmund's name. Picking up a marker, he put a star by power.

"Why that one?" she asked when he placed the marker back in its holder.

"It's the only one that makes sense. Edmund is a submissive male. There's often an odd dichotomy which is rarely explored in such a dynamic," he said, staring at the floor.

Jessica laid a hand on his shoulder. Everything in him wanted to pull away. There was nothing comfortable about the words he was about to express, but he knew there was truth in each one.

"That make no sense," Jessica said, turning toward him.

"It makes perfect sense and I mean no offense when I say it. A male submissive is both powerful and powerless. The sheer act of being male brings with it a set of expectations to be manly, strong, right and 'all knowing.' They wrote myths and fables about being a man. When you discover you want to submit, there's a push-pull dichotomy to it," he said shaking his head.

He watched her take in the information. It was the thing he'd struggled with the most when he realized his own inclinations.

Jessica nodded and stared at the white board. Across the room, he heard the door open as Ian strode in.

"What did you two figure out?" he asked as he joined them at the white board.

Kade watched as the realization hit him a few seconds later.

"You're not saying..." He paused.

Kade nodded.

"Shit," Ian swore softly.

"That seems to be the common reaction," Kade acknowledged with a deep sigh. "The question is can you help?"

Ian nodded. "How bad do you think it is?"

"I can't honestly say, but let's go on the presumption it's been going on for months and hope we are wrong."

"You really need to make sure housekeeping does a better job. I'll get a deep cleaning crew to sweep the corners and do a solid spring cleaning. Are there any annexes which might have been missed in Alexandra's absence?"

Kade shook his head at the coded message. He knew Ian's team would do a deep bug sweep of the club and the PR firm over the next two days. After they were comfortable all the rooms were clear of foreign surveillance devices, they'd make a plan to figure out how to contain the looming threat.

"Any idea on when Houdini might make an appearance?" Ian asked.

"I would give it a day or two. I can't imagine less than twenty-four hours. Do you think you'll be able to get housekeepers to clean up this mess before then?"

Ian grimaced. Kade knew it was a tight timeframe, but they needed to make sure that all the bugs were detected before Alexandra's return. The situation was already a clusterfuck, and he didn't need missed bugs on his conscience.

"It's a tight timeline, but I'll see what I can do."

Ian walked out the door as he brought the phone to his ear. The next twenty-four hours would make or break the club. Not only did they need to sweep for bugs, but they needed to keep the entire membership in the dark or there'd be a mass exodus of members.

Kade collapsed on the couch and placed his head in his hands. Guilt washed over him. Flashes of the last woman he couldn't save assaulted him as the situation exploded across his mind.

"Stop."

The command placed everything in his world on pause as he looked up into Jessica's stern, unyielding gaze.

"You can either take control of those memories, no matter how haunting or you can step aside and let us take care of the situation, but you can't do both at the same time."

He ran a hard hand through his hair. Anxiety leaned on every nerve and threatened to overtake him, but there was a strength in the woman in front of him. Kade knew with everything in him she'd take bullets for him both real and imaginary. For the first time in far too long he felt the glimmer of hope in the darkness of his own hell.

"What's next, Ma'am?"

"Next, we check on our guest and get some shut-eye. There's nothing else we can do here which will affect the outcome, and exhaustion won't help."

Kade knew she was right, but everything in him bristled at the idea of leaving his team in the middle of a situation.

"She's right," Tanner said from behind Kade.

He pivoted to face the man and came face to face with his Cheshire grin. They'd worked together far too long. Tanner had been on his team in the military and knew more about him than most people.

"Says the man who's not slept in, what, twenty-four hours?"

"I've slept. I've used the polyphasic sleep to keep me at the ready."

Kade sighed and shook his head.

"I could never understand your sleep schedule."

"You're jealous because I'm awake more and get more done," Tanner drawled.

"Yeah, let's go with that and not other reasons for your short sleep cycles. I presume you've got something or did you come here to be an annoying pain in the ass?"

"I thought being a pain in the ass was standard protocol based on your leadership." He grinned. "In all seriousness, I got a ping on that number you asked me to run earlier. We're triangulating the position now but none of us are experts in the field, and this guy is good at making sure we don't get a lock on him."

Kade looked down at the paper Tanner handed to him. He let out a sigh of annoyance at the lack of progress. There were several location circles, but none of them connected, and it had been over forty-eight hours since the last one.

He looked up and leveled a direct stare at Tanner like he was trying to assert his will over him.

"Find him. That's the mission. We're already past the time we should know the answer."

"Yes, Sir," Tanner said, taking the paper back from Kade.

"Let's go attend to our guest and get some shut-eye," he said without turning around toward Jessica.

"Glad you came up with such a brilliant plan."

Sarcasm dripped from her voice behind him. This was always where things broke down for him. There were times where he needed to take control and times when he needed to give it up. When they overlapped, he was never sure of the best way to handle it. Most dominant females never wanted to hear the word no, but he'd been lucky to have encountered some who understood the difference between fantasy and reality.

He took a deep breath and tried to find center in his tilting world.

"Reiterating your plan, Ma'am. We will move out at your leisure," he said. His body stiffened to attention.

Jessica's heels clicked and echoed around the room. When she rounded him, she looked up, and he could see the hint of a smile from his periphery.

"Nice save," she said and turned to head to the door.

Kade let out a harsh breath and fell in, two steps behind her and to her left.

THEY MADE THEIR WAY THROUGH THE CLUB AND DOWN TO THE area known affectionately as 'The Cell Block.' It was a series of three basic jail cells. The six by eight rooms were made of concrete block. In one corner was a stainless steel toilet and sink. There was a set of bunk beds with a thin mattress on each level on the opposite side of the room. Each guest was provided a pillow, two flat sheets, a washcloth, and a hand towel. Kade smiled at a few memories he'd had in this block.

As they rounded the corner, Cassandra shot up from the bed and rushed to the barred door. Her fingers wrapped in desperation as she pressed her face through the steel rods.

"You can't keep me here. This violates my rights. It's kidnapping," she shrieked.

He watched Jessica smile as she leaned against the wall opposite the cell door. The narrow corridor added to the illusion of the enclosed space.

"Yes and no, but we've already covered this ground, and I'm not really in the mood to cover it again. What I want to know is everything about your anonymous source. How they found you, what they wanted, if you ever talked to them on the phone."

Kade watched the seemingly casual conversation, but the undertone was unmistakable.

"I already wrote out everything I know."

"See, here's the thing, Cassandra, I don't think that's true. I think there's something you aren't telling us, and it's important."

Cassandra shook her head and stared at the floor.

"I've already told you everything I know. It was an anonymous contact. My assignment was to get into the club, take the Dominant mentor program, and write an article on the owner. Then all hell broke loose, and she disappeared," Cassandra said without meeting their gaze.

"If you were writing an article on Alexandra, why did you stay when she disappeared?"

Her foot drew a small circle on the concrete floor as her fingers drummed along the steel rods.

"Cassandra, Kade asked you a question," Jessica said.

She hesitated and drew in a deep breath. "It felt like home," she stated.

"Excuse me?" Jessica asked in confusion.

Cassandra's eyes shot up and her body stilled, as if she'd voiced something she'd been afraid to admit.

"The club... the people... everything. It felt like I belonged for the first time in my life. It was terrifying, exhilarating, confusing, and a thousand other things, but I couldn't go back to my old life. Not that I have anything to go back to," she said, dropping her gaze to the floor.

Kade wanted to reach out to Cassandra and tell her everything would be okay, but he wasn't sure it was true. Everything in her written 'confession' made him suspicious of her motivations.

"Do you think this is how a Dominant acts?"

Cassandra gave a tight laugh. "I don't know. I've watched pro Dominants come here and demand their way at every turn. I've watched husbands and wives walk in and immediately change their positions from the door to the bar. Then there's you, Detective. I can't figure you out. You don't raise your voice or demand anything, and yet people recognize you as a Dominant," Cassandra replied.

"There's no need to demand anything. Either a person follows me because they respect my leadership, skill, or the fact I'm really great at sex when I'm on top or they don't. Why force someone to be some-where they don't want to be?"

"But what if they like to be forced or controlled?" Cassandra blurted out.

Kade watched the shadow of emotions play across Jessica's face.

"As long as they are choosing it, then they should explore the rabbit hole as deep as they want to go. Get some sleep. We'll figure this mess out tomorrow," Jessica said, pushing off the wall.

"You can't leave me here!"

"Can and will. Think of it as an exploration of your perspective on helplessness and confinement," she said, a half smile pulling on her lips.

Without another word, Kade watched Jessica walk past him. Part of him wanted to comfort Cassandra, and another part was angry at her deceit. He was thankful he didn't have time to decide on which one to act on and followed Jessica out of the cell block.

CHAPTER TWENTY-EIGHT

J essica watched the crew work through the last of the public
areas with the bug detection devices. She was thankful they'd
finally gotten a few hours of sleep. Kade had wrapped his large
body around hers and she'd slept more soundly than she had done in
far too long. Her hands embraced the cup of coffee on the bar like it
was her lifeline. The late afternoon sun sank over the pool in hues of
orange and yellow. The long nights and short days were doing
nothing for her disposition.

"Can I top it off for you?" Jack asked, startling her out of her
thoughts.

She forced a smile and nodded then watched the dark liquid rise
between her hands.

"Looks like something major is going on around here," he said
with a nod toward one of the women with an electronic detector in
her hand.

"Yeah. Probably security maintenance," she said, bringing her cup
to her lips.

Jack wiped the bar with a towel, but the frown on his face told her he wasn't convinced. She hoped the membership took the excuse better than much of the staff.

"There you are," Kade said as he wrapped his arms around her.

"Someone is presumptuous today," she replied and pressed into him.

"What can I say? You are the place where I find balance, Ma'am."

Jessica laughed. "I'm not a place, Kade. You find balance all on your own."

He kissed the back of her neck.

"And well on your way to trouble if you continue down your current path," she said, biting back a moan.

"You two need to get a room," Samantha quipped as she walked up to the bar.

"We're in a BDSM club. The whole thing is a room," Kade dead-panned without releasing Jessica.

Samantha rolled her eyes before throwing Jessica a wink.

Across the club there was a stir of activity and the click of deter-mined heels on the stone floor.

"Kade! What have you done to my club?" A female voice echoed around the foyer.

Kade's entire body tensed. He released Jessica and turned toward the club's front door.

"Alexandra?" he asked in surprise. "We weren't expecting you back for a few more days."

Samantha jerked her head in the direction of the female walking toward them, and an elbow poked Kade in his ribs.

"How are..." Kade started to ask a question, but the woman's glare stopped him before he completed it. Jessica watched the interaction between the three.

"I take my PR Consultant, Atlas Devereaux, with me to scout for another location out of country, of which you were well aware, and you let this place go to hell in a hand basket in a matter of a couple months," she said as she shook her head in obvious disapproval.

Jessica looked around the spotless club and scowled. How dare she walk in here and tell Kade he was slacking on a job which was obviously done well? Every protective instinct surfaced, but she held back and watched as the woman worked through a myriad of emotions playing across her face.

"Well, if you were better at staying in touch, we might be able to run this place to your impossible standards," Kade challenged, making Jessica relax and smile.

"Watch your tone."

"My tone?" Kade replied.

"Yes. Or did you forget my position in the short time I was gone?"

Tension lay like a blanket in the air. Every muscle in Jessica's body tensed at the ready, but she forced herself to calmly slide off the barstool. Kade stepped forward into Alexandra's personal space, and Jessica braced for the confrontation. At the last second, she saw his head dip slightly and his body relax.

"It's good to see you too, Ma'am," Kade said right before he stepped forward and engulfed the woman in a bear hug.

When he stepped back, Jessica stepped around him to secure her place in the developing hierarchy.

"I don't believe we've met. I'm Jessica," she said, holding out her hand.

Alexandra glanced uncomfortably between her and Kade before offering a warm smile and a handshake.

"Jessica, this is Alexandra, the owner of this fine establishment. Alexandra, this is Detective Lawson. She's working the club's case," Kade said from behind her, an air of reverence in his voice.

"Shall we go to my office?" Alexandra offered. "Mr. Kinkaid, I presume the necessary reports are already on my desk."

"Yes, Ma'am, and more are being finished as we speak."

"Good. We've got quite a few things to discuss," she said and pivoted to walk down the hall.

Jessica stared at the back of the woman who'd turned the quiet of the club into a chaotic mess.

"Is she always like this?" Jessica asked.

"Don't let her brusque tone put you off," Samantha said as she walked up beside Kade. "Not everything is what it appears to be."

She watched Samantha follow Alexandra down the hall.

"Quite a bit of history between you two. I'd heard the stories, but the reality is different."

Kade turned to her.

"Yes, we've got quite a bit of history, but the important thing here is that I chose to follow you."

Kade tipped her chin up until she saw his eyes. Then he lowered his head and his mouth was on hers, telling her without words she was the one he wanted.

JESSICA FOLLOWED KADE DOWN THE HALL AND INTO Alexandra's office. Behind the massive desk, the woman looked exhausted. Dark circles hinted under her makeup, and she slouched like the world weighing on her was too much to bear.

"We weren't expecting you for a few more days," Kade said.

Alexandra nodded as Jessica watched them from the door.

"I see there are exterminators here. How bad?"

Kade shrugged. "Ian said he's seen worse."

She let out a strained laugh. "If Mr. Breckenridge used those terms, we're in trouble. I presume this office was cleared."

"Yes, Ma'am. It was the first thing on the list."

"Thank you. You've done an excellent job, Kade. I appreciate all of your hard work."

Jessica stared at the tone change between them. A few minutes earlier this same woman had almost berated Kade in front of the entire club, and now she gave him soft adoring praises. Alexandra's gaze turned toward her, and she stiffened.

"I also hear I am in your debt, Detective."

"Doing my job," she said.

For a long moment, Alexandra simply watched her. Under her scrutiny, Jessica shifted her weight.

"How did you enjoy my club?"

"It is beautiful," Jessica replied.

"Yet you are uncomfortable."

Her gaze moved between Kade and Alexandra.

"Thomas, could you give us a few minutes?" Alexandra asked without looking over at Kade.

Jessica watched Kade walk toward her and place a light kiss on her forehead.

"Good luck," he murmured as he walked out the office door.

When they were alone, Alexandra motioned to the seat in front of her desk.

"Please join me, Detective. I don't bite unless it is requested."

Jessica walked wearily over to the chair and sat, her back straight and body tense.

"Kade seems to have taken quite a liking to you," Alexandra stated.

"The feeling is mutual. I enjoy Mr. Kinkaid's company."

Alexandra leaned back, and Jessica felt like she was under a microscope.

"Let's see if I get my guess right," she started, steepling her fingers. "Someone or several of them have hurt you. Men have taken advantage of your size. The media tells you to be strong, and you think you are, but then you walk into this world and the practicum is harder than the theory."

Jessica nodded, stunned at the accuracy of Alexandra's words.

"And then you ran smack dab into Kade. This combination of self-assured and in need of center."

"He's... different."

"There's an understatement. Kade has been through hell on a couple different levels. From the looks of it, you both have your own unsteady ground. According to Samantha, you've struggled to settle into your dominant side."

Jessica scowled.

"It was a long plane ride back and I don't walk into unknown situations when the information is easy to gather," Alexandra said by way of explanation.

A smile tugged at the edges of Jessica's mouth.

"You aren't at all what I expected."

"I'm not surprised. The staff thinks I'm a bitch on wheels who doesn't tolerate excuses. My friends wonder at my sanity. To the outside world I'm the type of person who never hears 'no.'"

"Accurate."

"And you are a woman who's worked so hard to prove herself she doesn't know how to allow someone else to get the pickles off the top shelf rather than getting a step ladder."

Everything in Jessica wanted to argue, but the accuracy of the statement hit her with a solid resound.

"Everyone thinks intimacy is about the physical. All around my club people chase it. But it's really about truth. Being able to open and tell someone your truth. To know you are both safe together. It's part of a power exchange. The hardest part. To know as a Dominant you are as vulnerable as the submissive you lead."

"How?" The question stuck in Jessica's throat.

"Practice. Failure. Rinse. Repeat."

"I adore him."

"That much is obvious. Now quit second-guessing yourself because you're trying to live up to some ideal. I've not seen Kade light up like he does for you in far too long."

"KADE," SHE SAID AS SHE ENTERED HIS OFFICE.

He rose from behind his own desk and nodded to her. "Yes, Ma'am?"

"I want to know one thing. Is this what you want or was it all part of the fantasy this club exudes?"

Kade walked around his desk until he stood in front of her. He cupped her face between his large hands and forced her to look up at him.

"You are who I follow."

"Even when I stumble in the dark not knowing the next steps to take? When the world questions my authority because of my size or gender?"

"Especially then. An exchange means we are both in it. The weight is not only on you or only on me... it's on us. There's no specific way for any of this to go but how we choose it."

Jessica looked into his eyes for a long minute, finding her own strength in his.

"Kneel," she commanded, her tone soft and warm.

He smiled, released her face, and fell to his knees in a kneel up position. Here, they were closest they ever could be to a similar height.

"You know, I still owe you for biting me without permission. And then there was the quip about fucking me in the ass," she said, schooling the emotions on her face.

"Yes, Ma'am," Kade said with enthusiasm.

Jessica laughed. "I want to be everything you want in a Dominant."

"There's no list. It's about mutual benefit and pleasure, besides you may find my cock buried deep in your ass is exactly what you want."

A mischievous grin played across his face as he moved his hands to grip her ass and pulled her closer.

"Did I give you permission to grab my ass?"

Kade tried to look contrite, but failed.

"No, Ma'am, but it is such a beautiful ass, how am I supposed to resist?"

She bent slightly and ran a thumb across his lips. Her fingers slid into his mouth as he teased them with his tongue.

"You know, this tongue of yours will get you into trouble," she said, pinching it between her fingers then releasing it when he groaned.

"It's also been known to be a source of great pleasure and satisfaction, as I recall."

Jessica gave a breathy moan at the memory of his tongue working over her clit. She knew her power over him was equal to his over her and relaxed in their banter. He was more experienced in the lifestyle, and yet he let her take the lead. There was so much to learn, and in this moment she knew they would both enjoy every minute.

"Maybe we should put it to the test. A repeat performance. As I recall, you weren't allowed to come after our encounter. It will take several days for the bite mark to heal. In return, you can pleasure me several times a day over that same time period but won't be allowed a release. I think it will be enough to make up for my 'pain and suffering' while reminding you to ask next time," she said.

Kade's head dropped at her pronouncement, and when he looked up, there was a glint in his eyes.

"If I understand you, then it will be a requirement to pleasure you several times a day, but I may not release. Is this correct?"

Jessica nodded.

"Lesson one—a Dominant should always be specific. I think it's time you learn this game goes both ways," he said, a grin tugging at the corners of his mouth.

His fingers reached up to work the button of her pants.

"What are you doing?"

"Pleasuring you, for the first of several times today. You weren't specific, and I thought we'd get started."

When her pants and panties hit the floor, he nuzzled the inside of her thigh as he explored her with his lips, teasing her slit as he worked his tongue into her folds.

"What if someone walks in?"

Kade paused and looked up at her with a smile. "Then they walk in. Next time you should lock the door, Mistress."

There was no time for her to form a reply as a bold swipe of his tongue sent her spinning into a soft swirl of pleasure.

EPILOGUE

"**G**ood afternoon, everyone." Alexandra addressed the group from behind her desk, looking around the room to the people who'd saved her life.

Ian and Jillian stood near the door while Jessica and Kade sat in the chairs in front of the large desk. Over to the right, Samantha sat in the office chair they'd pulled from Katie's desk. Every person watched her from their positions in the room.

"First, thank you. I owe every one of you a great debt. It is one I can never repay. Faced with my poor decisions, you rallied to not only save my life, but also this club. Based on everything we know, I think we are better equipped to end this game once and for all. Once we locate Dominick, we can concentrate all of our focus on the situation at hand," she said. "We need to get everything back on track, so we can get back to business."

Alexandra shifted in her seat.

"I hear you've been looking for me," Dominick said, his deep voice resonating around the office.

Every person in the room turned and gawked at him.

"Where the hell have you been?" Alexandra demanded as she rose from behind the desk.

Dominick held up his hand, and she immediately went silent.

"Working. There are other things in play here."

He stepped into the office, and bodies moved out of his way as he stepped in front of Alexandra's desk.

"I am glad you are safe. I was worried," Alexandra said. She glanced toward the floor and immediately brought her gaze back to his.

"I understand you've been through quite the ordeal yourself. My sources tell me Reece should make a full recovery, though it will be a long one."

"Your sources?" Kade asked from behind him.

"Yes, Thomas. There's an advantage to knowing everything. A power in it, you might say."

"The question is why do you need power?" Jessica asked.

Dominick turned toward her.

"I don't think I've had the pleasure of your acquaintance."

"No, Mr. Dawes, you have not," she said without further elaboration.

Dominick chuckled. "I like you, Detective," he said, turning back to Alexandra.

"How did you know..."

"Patience, Detective. All things in good time. Now, I understand Cassandra is being confined on the grounds. Since I'm the one who put her here, I would like to see her."

A scowl crossed Alexandra's face.

"What do you mean you put her here?"

Dominick sighed. "I don't think it is hard to understand. You know she had an anonymous source. I am that source. I gave her the job which put her in your club, and I would like to see her now."

The tension in the room was palpable as Dominick and Alexandra both stood their ground.

Ian cleared his throat from near the door. "Mr. Dawes, if you will follow me to the cell block, I'll take you to Cassandra."

A smile formed across Dominick's stern face.

"You placed her in the cell block?" he asked.

"Yes. Based on the information we received in our ongoing investigation, we thought it was the best place to keep her... safe," Jessica replied.

Dominic turned and faced Jessica.

"Aren't you full of surprises? Maybe all of this will work after all," he said with a nod. "Now, please take me to Cassandra."

They all watched as Dominick walked to the door as he followed Ian out toward the club.

ABOUT THE AUTHOR

Sappharia Mayer's erotic romance comes from years of experience in dynamic and various play in the BDSM/Kink lifestyle. She portrays the dance of power exchange relationships with a passion that pushes her characters, and readers, outside their comfort zone, making them squirm, cry, laugh and learn to see things in a whole new way.

Living around the metro area of the nation's capital gives her an up close view of politics and power on a global scale. She loves to delve deep into her worlds and indulge in her various passions, which may or may not include instigating fun *trouble* with her warped sense of humor. If you love romance with based in power exchanges with hot kinky sex, then check out Sappharia's books.

PLEA FROM THE AUTHOR

I am so glad you've reached the end of the book and hope you enjoyed it. Thank you for giving me your valuable entertainment time. It is readers like you who make writing such an amazing experience.

If you enjoyed the book, I hope you will leave a review.

Be the First to Know

Want news, pre-order announcements or stuff?

www.SapphariaMayer.com

Want to catch up on all my behind the scenes, current WIPs, side projects and early announcements? Become a Patreon of the Arts.

Sappharia Mayer's Patreons of the Arts

Feel free to reach out to me on any of my social media.

BB bookhub.com/authors/sappharia-mayer

twitter.com/sapphariamayer

pinterest.com/sapphariamayer

amazon.com/author/sapphariamayer

instagram.com/sapphariamayer

PLAY WITH ME- CHAPTER 1
EMPYREAN CLUB- THE ATLAS COLLECTION BOOK 5

There is an eery calm. Emotions recede. A deep breath comes. My voice is but a whisper. The cool crisp of logic infuses itself into every pore. Details I would let go mere minutes ago are now important. Each one better be perfect. For greater men than you have beat the emotions out of me until all I knew was perfection through annihilation.

Emotion is illogical. It takes much to get me to the place where I am open and they flow freely. I must work to be open, no matter how much I desire to do so. It is a labor.

The fastest way usually comes when I have failed, for they use emotions to beat me into submission. The crashing waves of all the things I've missed all of my failure and realization of my worst fears. Under it, my knees buckle and I release.

I want there to be another way, but too many situations, too many people use it against me. Release is sometimes such a wonderful thing. Other times it stokes a different fire. It is all in the path to get there and the safety I find.

But now... now is not the path of positive positions. Now is the path past anger. Filled with protection. Focused from the words beginning to whisper through my thoughts. "Emotions make you weak." "Keep this up and you will prove the failure I already know you are." "No one wants to be with an emotional woman!" "So men are better, they are stoic and strong." "Women are less because they use emotions to manipulate situations." "Men are always more successful because they logical and can think in a crisis."

I've heard them all and then some. There were times I hit my knees and did not think I would get up as the emotions swirls through me. Then I learned the cold, cruel calculation of logical thought. It does not care about you nor does it attach any emotion to your situation. Through its lens, you are an object who threatens to harm my world. Every fuzzy detail becomes clear. Question more pointed. My entire world is a deep breath of calm. My patience is thin and observation is even higher than normal. Here, I will take mass casualties to ensure damage because yours will match mine. It is a game of chicken, chess and go. Each one with a different aim and strategy.

My voice is now but a whisper, as a smile slides across my face. Harm to one I love now ends my level of patience, anger and sleepless nights it cost me to get here again. Every lesson I've learned now trains every skill on one goal. Your move. Greed got you here. Emotions can't save you. And I've got lots of time- do you?

I'll send your regards to the men who taught me those lessons before you.

Emotions are weakness and I am not.

THE KNOCK AT THE DOOR DRAWS MY ATTENTION, BUT I DO NOT look up.

"Enter," I command, my pen finishing the last strokes with a flourish.

Katie enters the room and sets a cup of coffee on my desk, then picks up the cold one.

"My apologies for the interruption, ma'am. Mr. Kinkaid is here to see you."

"Tell him I will find him later."

"She'll tell me no such thing," Kade says, his voice booming in an echo around the room. "You've scurried between three locations at all hours for the last month. We've all give you time and space, but enough is enough, Ma'am."

I lift my eyes. He stands in a perfect parade rest. His eyes forward in respect. Tension ripples through his muscles.

"I've got businesses to run, Thomas. He put my life, and the lives of others, in danger and on hold with his games. It left everything in shambles. Now, I must catch up before it all falls apart," I reply with an icy tone as I place the fountain pen on top of the journal entry I was writing.

"With all due respect, you are surrounded with a capable team."

"You are all capable, but it is my responsibility. It stops on my desk. Every detail, every decision comes from me. No matter if I make them or not. Both as a dominant and as a business owner," I say and push my chair back from the desk. The space is suddenly confining.

"If you'd continued to build your team, this situation would be easier," Dominick replies as he walks through the door. "I always thought Thomas would make a fine Major Domo and from the looks of this place, he was doing an excellent job at running your House while you were... indisposed."

"Dominick," I acknowledge.

I watch his eyebrow raise in a question but he does not verbalize it.

"This isn't your concern," I continue. "Mr. Kinkaid ran the club, and some of its major events, with efficiency, but it is my understanding he struggled under the stress and the weight of them. It is unfair, as the head of this House- or club as it is in actuality, to unduly place such weight on the staff."

Kade does not move as Dominick walks behind him.

243

"I don't disagree that you failed. If you'd continued the correct course of training, provided the necessary skills to Mr. Kinkaid and the other staff members, the burden would not be as heavy. However, you chose this direction by your own actions. Now, you must train others to take control and while you learn to release it in the most dire times. A troublesome situation without doubt," Dominick says as he lowers himself into the chair to my right in front of the desk.

I pull my shoulders back and straighten. This is a battle of wills, and Dominick has a clear advantage of position and history.

"It's not your call," I state. "Mr. Kinkaid is capable. You are correct that I should expand his training in this job when the timing is better. For the moment, I am more than able to right this ship, so to speak."

"Pardon my disagreement," Ian says from the doorway.

I take a deep breath and sigh.

"As a fiscal investor in this enterprise," he says as his arms motion to the room and club, "I am in agreement with these two gentlemen."

"You are a thirty percent investor," I remind him.

"Fifty-two. Your absence caused a need for an influx of funds in several divisions of your enterprise and I stepped in to help," Ian replies as he takes the seat beside Dominick.

Kade cringes.

"I'll discuss this with you later, Kade," I say through clenched teeth.

I take a deep breath to calm the swirl of emotions and reach for the next logical step.

"Gentlemen," I address them, "I appreciate your concern. Mr. Breckenridge, I will be glad to discuss our current business arrangements enacted in my absence. Mr. Dawes, your personal insertion into this matter has caused quite enough issues. Mr. Kinkaid, you and I will discuss your decisions at length. Now, if you all will excuse me, there is a mountain of work which requires my attention."

"You're southern hospitality is slipping. Along with its accent," Samantha quips as she walks into the office. "Just accept the help."

"Why does this feel like an ambush?"

"More like an intervention," Dr. Jillian Hart replies as she enters.

"Out! All of you. This is my office and my realm," I command.

"Hear us out, Alexandra. Give us an hour. We're here to help," Jillian replied and stepped towards my desk.

I close my eyes and try to find my center. Work is my solace, even if it overwhelms me right now. All I need is for them to get out and let me do my job.

Pain radiates up my neck as the headache, which was building moments before, takes hold. I refuse to rub my temples, not giving them another inch into my world. I open my eyes, glance down at my desk and center myself. With the last draw of strength, I smile and stand, pulling myself up to a perfect posture.

"Thank you all for your concern. This situation is tough for everyone of us, in different ways. I never intended to affect you and an apology is far too little, too late. All I can do is ask for your forgiveness and patience," I say as focus on maintaining the deep southern accent indicative of Alexandra.

"Sit down," Dominick says in a menacing whisper. He hands Kade an envelope.

Kade steps forward, places it on my desk and steps back to his original position.

"Take those before that headache of yours gets worse," Dominick nods to the envelope on my desk. "We expect you in the studio apartment above the PR firm in an hour. Failure to make the appointment in the appropriate 'identity' will be met with dire consequences. Do not push me on this, Alexandra."

Everyone nods in agreement. I focus an icy glare at Dominick. Nothing escapes his observation, and my frustration grows at the inability to hide the smallest issues.

"Not advisable," he states. "We'll see you in an hour."

Without another word, he stands and walks out the door. The rest of the group follows until only Samantha is left.

"How are you?" She asks, her tone soft and full of concern.

"I'm fine. There's a mountain of work, but I'll get it done or undone, whichever is more appropriate."

"Why?"

The simple question punches straight into my gut. It is laced with accusations and betrayal.

"My job is to protect you. All of you. No matter the cost," I reply in resignation.

"That's stupid."

I shake my head. "It's not. My personal honor code and duty call me to it."

"Your code is flawed. It's missing an important piece. One I am unsure how you've not learned," she whispers.

"And what is my code missing?"

"Family. Community. The acknowledgement of the people around you who care for you. All of them are smart, intelligent, talented and capable. It isn't you against the world, Alexandra. It is all of us pulling together and making it work. We all have difficulties. Every person here is full of strengths and weaknesses," Samantha continues. "How does an amazing dominant and wicked smart business owner miss such a thing?"

"I see you've been hanging around Dominick too much," I try to joke.

"Yes. He's worried about you. We all are, but he's especially so."

"He gave up the right to worry about me when I moved to DC."

"Actually, you gave it back to him when you went to his brownstone for help. There's more to that man than meets the eye," Samantha says, as she furrows her brow.

"I owe him a debt, but I am not his responsibility."

"First, I don't think he sees it that way. There's something about the entire thing which feels... off."

Curiosity blooms. Samantha's knowledge of Dominick runs as

deep as mine, but he's always been a mystery to me, no matter how close we were.

"Off... how?"

"I don't know. There's something he's not saying and the whole thing with Cassandra is just... odd," she says as she stood and shook her head. "Maybe I'm trying to make something out of nothing."

Samantha shrugged.

"An intervention? Really?" I ask, as Samantha walks toward the door.

"Yes. Really," she says over her shoulder as she leaves the office.

The headache blooms. I idly pick up the envelope as I stare out the window.

"I'm so tired of ambushes," I mutter.

PLAY WITH ME (THE ATLAS COLLECTION BOOK 5)

Buy Play with Me *Today!*

ALSO BY SAPPHARIA MAYER

EMPYREAN CLUB SERIES

The Atlas Collection

Mask Me (Book 1)

Master Me (Book 2)

Reveal me (Book 3)

Submit to Me (Book 4)

Play with Me (Book 5)

Mind Games Series

His Toy Collection

Becoming His Toy

His Toy for the Weekend

His Toy is Going Deeper

His Toy is Trusting Him

ABOUT THE AUTHOR

Sappharia Mayer's erotic romance comes from years of experience in dynamic and various play in the BDSM/Kink lifestyle. She portrays the dance of power exchange relationships with a passion that pushes her characters, and readers, outside their comfort zone, making them squirm, cry, laugh and learn to see things in a whole new way.

Living around the metro area of the nation's capital gives her an up close view of politics and power on a global scale. She loves to delve deep into her worlds and indulge in her various passions, which may or may not include instigating fun *trouble* with her warped sense of humor. If you love romance based in power exchanges with hot kinky sex, then check out Sappharia's books.

www.ingramcontent.com/pod-product-compliance
Lightning Source LLC
Chambersburg PA
CBHW020358210626
46816CB00006BB/2024